Through the Whirlpool

Book I
OF
Seeking the Jewel Fish

K. Eastkott

Seeking the Jewel Fish

Through the Whirlpool

Book 1 of
Seeking the Jewel Fish

K. Eastkott

Escapade Press

(an imprint of)

POBLESECBOOKS

Published by Escapade Press, an imprint of Poble Sec Books, in 2017. First published as an e-book in 2013.

British Library Cataloguing in Publication Data

A CIP catalogue record for this book is available from the British Library.

www.poblesecbooks.com

ISBN: (print) 9780957655171; (.epub) 9780957655126

FOR RIA.

I.
THE SEA CALLER

After the chill pre-dawn, the heat, as she breasted the summit, buffeted her, almost throwing the old woman back downhill. During the final thousand paces of the climb, the ground had gradually warmed then scorched the soles of her feet through her thin sandals. Now sweat poured from her body and she dreamed of a cool place, some crystal mountain stream where she might sit and soak her tired legs. Such was not to be found on Kaa-meergeh. The entire island was barren red rock. And her task was not to rest but to prompt, encourage, coerce — at times threaten, or worse. First among the shahiroh, the sea callers, she was there to supervise the rite, there for sea-nomad-becoming.

Braving the heat, she forced herself again toward the crater and stood on its very lip.

"Taashou!"

The distant shout barely penetrated the deafening grind of the lava's music, and she ignored it, forcing her sight down into the lava lake, which tossed its bright spears high. Despite the flames, Kaa-meer-geh was at peace, its magma pulsating warm ruby calm encrusted with dark rock scabs.

She bore the heat. Slim, athletic, her body taut skin over toned muscles. Random streaks shone silver in her plaited hair, belying a strength honed with the years. Against the rough basalt, she resembled the ancient trunk of a loman tree, polished and elegant.

In trance she waited, allowing her prescience to roll down into the molten stone and through it to that fluid intermingling of time and space where the universe ground against other dimensions. Future and past possibilities—crackling snakes of time—inter-wove and sparked off one another. Then the rock flames brought her a single vision: a figure writhing far above, engulfed in flames as it fell toward midnight waves. Though no screams reached her, still she knew who... She fought to hold the sight... And her heart lurched as the victim disappeared beneath the ocean's surface.

"Taashou!"

That shout broke the trance, dissolving the ocean into fire. Golden stanzas seemed to shimmer in the heat-drenched air even as the sight dissipated:

The foreign seeker will be lost,
An ocean's guardian laid low,
Before the one of touch afar
Restores a peace from long ago.

The strange prophecy seemed to echo a time long before when something else had emerged from the magma.

Her concentration had been shattered by that distant cry. She turned to face the horizon. The sea lay dark: a pan of murky oil awaiting a taper. Here and there, long swathes of water gleamed: the kree-eh—primeval life forms that glowed phosphorescent in its depths. A few final stars above were fading like sparks on the breeze. Dawn was near. She searched for whoever was calling her name, but the volcano's slopes lay in gloom and she could see no movement below.

From her belt, she unslung two objects and laid them on the sand: one a carved mask, its features defying description. Seeming to breathe as if alive, it sighed—a heritage ground out of rocks. It held its mystery to itself. Not yet time for its secrets to emerge.

The woman picked up the other, an arm-long, twisting shell. Fluted fingers flowered from a conical opening. It had a rough exterior of deepest purple but inside shone like sunrise. Another shout from below. She ignored it again. There would be time to address it later. For thirty-two years, this had been her role and none had dared to interrupt; they would not do so now. So it was that pride condemned her to her dearest mistake.

On the horizon, gray dawn softened into lilac, from there to indigo and copper. Celestial depths chameleoned into gold. Though almost full daylight up here, below the beach lay dark. Then a sparkle at the sea's far reach, and the sun's fire leaped above the horizon.

She put the shell horn to her lips—hesitated—and

blew. A high, sad wail drifted out, gliding away over the island as the sun floated up into the sky, its rays saluting. The trumpet call rolled down the volcano's slopes as far as the barren shore and outward over the ocean beyond. Moments later, an answering wail—a fading moan from the mainland shadows. Seven horn blasts in total sounded from the mainland. Sea-nomad-becoming had commenced.

"Taashou, wait!"

Lowering the horn, she peered down into the predawn gloom. A figure was toiling up the slope, close now. It was Lehd, youngest of the sea callers, he whose shouts had meant to distract her.

"We shouldn't have started," he panted. "It is… too dangerous. The others have seen it… sent me to tell you… the rift has opened!"

If he could have seen her expression... but from where he was standing her figure flickered ghostlike in the volcano's hot embrace. He knew she was angry with him for interrupting the ritual, but he could not see that shadow sliding across her face as she turned back to the fire, its highest flames now invisible in the sunlight. Her thoughts were her own as she pondered the rift... So it had returned. But where would it lead them this time?

2.
SEA-NOMAD-BECOMING

Night receded, lifting him from sleep. In the silence—as still as the polished surface of a moonlit lake—some whisper had nudged him in his dreams. His fingers reached for the leather bag looped on a thong around his throat, caressing a hidden shape. Yet there were only the sounds of every night: the rolling crash of surf on the beach, soothing, repetitive; and a hissing rattle that flapped around their hut like a clumsy bird—the wind clattering the palms. The surf ebbed and broke almost in time with his parents' breathing—a guttural snore and a gentle whistling—both rhythms entwined in their own melody. These were the comfortable sounds of his world—so familiar he had to listen carefully to pick them out. It was something else, a subtle scratching of claws on the walls of his mind. Then other mental noise intruded. People had begun to awake. The village was stirring.

He sat up, remembering what must be begun, where he was headed today. He was ready. Stretching limbs and cracking joints, he shook off sleep, threw aside his blanket, relishing the predawn chill. He washed his face. As he ran through his exercises, he heard his father's feet hit the floor with a slap as he too rolled from his hammock. His mother groaned, imaged a sleepy question, but his father replied in words: "Sea-nomad-becoming."

Sunrise was close. Finishing his exercises, he closed his eyes for a moment. Sea-nomad-becoming. Today he would shed his former life. Tomorrow he might be a man.

A mind question from his mother…

No. Later he could eat. The rites demanded that he fast until arrival. Zjhuud-geh Island would be teeming with fruit, and he was capable with a snare, handy with a fishing spear and line. Food gathered by his own hand… that would be the easiest part. His mother pushed aside the curtain defining his personal space and placed a full gourd beside his tools. This was the only sustenance he could carry. A potion of herbs steeped in a mother's knowledge. A life source.

He spent a few moments checking his tools, though they had been polished, sharpened, repaired repeatedly over the last week and were as honed as could be. He was wrapping them, securing them in their woven bag when it came: a faint, high moan floating across the sea, from Kaa-meer-geh Island… the summons. Another call rose in answer. Closer this time, down on the beach. The call of the sea, inviting him, Kreh-ursh, and his friends to embark on sea-nomad-becoming. The long wail died away, then sounded again moments later. And again. He held his breath: seven horn blasts. Seven hopefuls about to set off. Seven… who should have been eight. Kaar-oh, his friend, who had trained with him, would never attempt the nomad-becoming now.

Perhaps it was wrong, but the impulse was too great. Kreh-ursh stooped into a corner and opened a wooden chest. He took out a tiny leather bag, similar to his own yellow one but crimson. Inside, another unique carved shape, which only he had looked at since... it had been his friend's. He hung this second bag around his neck too. The best he could do. Might Kaar-oh know. Then it was as if, in his imagination, he felt his friend stir, breathe again. He heard his laugh, found himself smiling at the gap-toothed grin... Crazy!

Looking around his small section of the hut, he surveyed it all—hammock, chest, floor mat, spears, fishing tackle, wooden toys from when he was a boy—a pile of things, so important once. Nothing he would take now. He tightened his belt from which the gourd and his knife hung, shouldered the heavy bundle containing his tools, cooking utensils and a few other belongings, slung blanket and sleeping mat across his back, and ducked under the curtain.

In the family space, his parents were waiting for him. His mother smiled tightly as she hugged him, though he sensed her tears. His father's frown shielded his feelings as he too embraced his son.

"Just follow what you learned at training. Good luck."

This was it. Kreh-ursh left the hut, heading for the beach. Sea-nomad-becoming had begun.

3.
BEGINNING THE DREAMING

Barely was she out of bed before Jade was reaching for her wetsuit in the dark. The clammy neoprene was still damp from the day before and, as she pulled it on over her swimsuit, she thought about her mother's words. It was true she was not supposed to go by herself, but this sunrise ritual was one she just had to complete alone. Besides, of her mates, neither Miguel nor Darren would be up this early.

Creeping downstairs, she left the house quietly, and grabbed her board from where it was leaning against the side of the house. After a short walk down the road and through the dunes, she was soon on the beach, which was deserted at that hour. The sand felt pleasantly cool under her toes, but the surf, as she pounded into it in a rush, hit her like ice after her warm bed.

Mauri Cove, known as a fairly safe, east-coast beach, was protected from the full anger of the ocean swell to the north by Pine Bluff's looming bulk and the outflow of the Mauri River. To the south, Mauri Point speared the ocean eastward, with the lighthouse crowning its tip. Between these two arms, a long stretch of water produced some of the best surf on the entire coast.

Paddling out to where the waves rolling into the bay heaped themselves into long, arching ridges as they rounded the point, she sat on her board and waited. Rank upon rank of those blue-gray hills stretched to the choppy horizon. When the sun came up, it transmuted the water to gold before her. This was the perfect moment in her entire day. The only features marring the view east were three pale, distant towers. Though resembling an oil rig, they were in fact a new research station for some sort of ecological fuel that was being developed.

Once she could feel the sun on her face, Jade turned her board and, searching for the first wave of the day, which had to be perfect, began to surf. The larger waves were breaking at the north end of the beach, close to where the Mauri River emptied into the bay. It was a tricky place to surf because of the turbulence the river caused, and she needed all her concentration.

Ten minutes or so later, she had just jumped off her board in the shallows to head for deep water again, when her attention was caught by the sound of a speedboat. The early hour, plus the direction it came from, seemed strange. Glancing over her shoulder as she crested a wave, she saw a slick, fiberglass craft come skimming around a bend in the Mauri River. It bumped across the rapids at the river mouth, and aimed straight for the open sea. As it passed her, sunlight reflected off its windshield and she could not see the vessel's occupants. She forgot all about it, and kept paddling out to where she could catch her next wave.

With her attention focused on the surfing conditions, she

did not notice the speedboat's return, half an hour later, until it was almost too late. Cresting a wave, she found the craft's shining bow bearing down on top of her.

"Hey! Watch it!"

The driver saw her and swung the wheel hard left. Jade threw herself to her left also, but there was a *clunk* as her board smashed against the vessel's hull. Something sloshed from a tank on board. Then Jade was underwater, trying to kick back away from the launch's spinning propeller. Multicolored ribbons of some sort of seaweed filled the water around her, clinging to her body and twining through her hair.

When she broke water, a strange taste filled her mouth, something other than the saltiness of the sea. She also heard a familiar voice:

"It's Weasel! Hey brat, I'm coming for ya!"

That was when she recognized the boat's occupants: Rena, accompanied by her two cronies. Jade knew she was in trouble. Some years older than Jade, Rena worked as the security guard up at the new lab. That was where they had first clashed. To Jade, Darren and Miguel, it had seemed fun at the time to tease her, careering around in the darkness on the half-built site, trying to stay ahead of Rena's torch beam. That was until the day Miguel, had "fallen" from his bike out by Point Mauri and broken his arm. Jade now knew that Rena was bad news. Beside her in the speedboat sat the Head, a thick-shouldered boy of limited intelligence but unswerving loyalty to her, and Screwdriver, a rat-faced youth, who was steering.

Pulling herself onto her board, she began to paddle furiously, expecting to hear the craft gaining on her. Yet when she threw a glance back, the launch had turned and resumed its course for the river mouth.

Once it had gone, she sat on her board and thought. Her hankering for surfing had disappeared, and she began to paddle slowly shoreward. It was strange that the gang had not chased her. What might be more important to that crew than settling their score with her when they had her there, trapped in the water? It must be some shady job they could not afford to delay.

She was swimming. Deep in the green, beneath the waves, far down where massive blocks of stone piled in weighty majesty to create palaces. She was swimming. Clouds of sparkling color surrounded her like ribbons of fine sea kelp. Yet this stuff seemed aware, sentient. She felt it brush against her as she propelled herself forward and ever downward through the green… through the phosphorescence… and almost felt its whispered thoughts. Far off, sea creatures wailed and moaned, distracting her with their guttural syllables that sounded so achingly familiar.

Somehow she knew they were singing for her, but she could not understand their tongue.

"Jade!"

This time the voice was human, someone calling from far away. She knew it was just a dream. Yet like no other. Still she swam, wanting to dive deeper, down toward the kelp voices, careening through the green…

"Jaa-aade!"

She was being pulled from the depths, but the clouds of kelp—lilac, red, green, and silver—were also calling, pulling her backward. She had to leave… but those voices again, were speaking… to her almost. As if she had caught their meaning but could not quite remember. This was important, something about colors that could save her, save someone, but she was being pulled up. A strange boy's laugh trilled long, taunting her. Everything else began to fade. All gone except for that echoing laugh, mocking her because she could not stay. His disdain held a note of frenzy she distrusted.

"Jade!"

She opened her eyes to see Kyle, oversized boogie board under his arm, standing beside her towel.

"Mom's on her way, it's high tide. Come on, there's surf!"

The waves rolling in were high. She was on the beach, lying on her towel. Kyle was staring at her with as much concern as a kid brother could muster, more wrapped up in his own predicament: missing all those beautiful rollers that were surging into Mauri Cove.

"Chill. If you go in before Mom gets here, we'll be having barbecued Kyle for dinner, I promise."

She sat up, trying to organize her thoughts, bring herself back into the present. It had happened again, the strange dream or nightmare, almost as if she were there, so real it seemed. Kyle flopped down beside her.

"I'll never learn to surf if I have to sit here on the beach all the time! What's taking her so long?"

"The usual. One of her clients called. Some company wants to gut some old mansion. Mom's getting an injunction."

She did not bother to explain "injunction" to her brother's raised eyebrows. Four years younger than Jade, if she was not sure, Kyle would have no clue. She wanted to go in surfing as well. The thought of the spray crashing as you sped down the waves like some goddess of the ocean—it cured everything. On her own she might, but with Kyle there, she would definitely be dragged through seven separate kinds of hell.

She lay back again. Closing her eyes, she concentrated on the buzzing red behind her eyelids... This dream: for a week now these spells had been recurring, calling her down to dive deep into the green among those colored ribbons. Afterwards, she would shiver and feel deathly cold as if she were lying on the ocean floor deep down… like a disabled submarine on the seabed. And that chanting, the laughter… It was as if she were being challenged, or summoned... Those haunting syllables and a boy's cruel laughter. She had no idea what it meant, but the colors were so beautiful—like every hue wrapped together—a silky matter that floated deliciously in the depths… And then this dizziness…

A shadow blocked the sun as she lay on her towel. Squinting against the light, she peered up. And her heart stopped. Unused to seeing the blubbery body out of uniform, dressed only in beach shorts and a tee, one arm wrapped around her board, Jade could still not mistake the sadistic glint in those eyes. The older girl may have let her prey slip away a week ago, but this time Jade knew she would not be so lucky. She had no escape… and Kyle was right beside her.

"What do you want, Rena?"

The older girl scowled: "You, Weasel. I want you!"

4.
EMBARKING

When Kreh-ursh arrived at the beach, seven of the blue-robed shahiroh—the sea callers, those most powerful chanters among the sea nomads—were standing in a group. A short distance beyond, his village's proudest possession, the great canoe, was pulled up at the tidemark. The length of fifteen men lying end to end, and so wide a sailor could sleep across one of its benches, it dominated the sand, dwarfing the beached fishing canoes alongside. Capricious magic flowed from the intricate designs in its high, carved prow and stern, tingling with life, demanding respect.

A crew of forty or so Shahee, or sea nomads, clothed in their customary green, stood beside it. At a distance from them, six pale-robed candidates, all weighed down by packs and blankets like himself—four girls and two boys—huddled into cloaks against the dawn chill. As he approached, only Geh-meer broke her tense concentration to flash him one of her brief smiles. The others just looked nervous, unwilling to talk.

"Ready?"

"I don't think so. Is it too late to pull out?"

She smiled again. "You know you wouldn't. We'll be fine."

Her words, sparse as they were, comforted. Once on the island, they would be alone, bound to silence—mental and verbal—reliant only on their own skill. If and when they returned, the celebration would be memorable, but that was a world away, on the far side of this test.

It had been a harsh year: climbing jungle slopes; swimming tiring stretches against the current; cutting, shaping, and carving heavy logs; being tossed together in a flimsy canoe on treacherous Shah—the wide sea. Together the eight of them had fought to master the sea nomad's five skills. Mind speech, the most important of these, was how his people spoke to each other, the Shahee sea nomads with easy precision, but the shahiroh sea callers as true adepts. Next, candidates had to know how to read the sky and waves for the information they could reveal. Wavecrafting, the third skill, meant shaping ocean currents, literally bending water. Akin to that was windcalling, harnessing the rhythms of the air to do one's bidding; finally, though not least, came woodworking and carving, learning to feel for the life within growing things, especially the trees, and mold it to one's purpose.

These five skills, along with adherence to the life code, or unwavering respect for all living things, was the backbone of Shahee heritage. Shah, the eastern sea, was their home. Though voluntary, sea-nomad-becoming should be undertaken only when one was ready, and Kreh-ursh would rather perish than fail this test. His future, he knew, was with the Shahee, his people. Any other alternative was unthinkable.

On the shingle above the high tide mark, a crowd had gathered. Kreh-ursh spied his parents and waved, then stopped, unsure if that seemed too childish for this moment. Then he saw her, another figure standing apart, her loneliness like a shout against the strong group feeling shared by the village. Their eyes met. She tried to smile, but merely prompted his own tears to swell. He swallowed, biting back guilt, rage, many things he could not express. However, he showed her, pulling the scarlet leather pouch from his tunic so the boy's mother would know: Kaar-oh might yet complete sea-nomad-becoming, symbolically, if not in fact.

"It is time!"

At the shahiroh's cry, Kreh-ursh, Geh-meer, and the other candidates walked down to the water's edge. The wet sand felt cold underfoot. The Shahee placed themselves on either side of the heavy vessel, and, as the shahiroh began to chant, they added their voices. Sacred syllables spilled into the crisp dawn. Energy rippled from the chanting sea callers to the great canoe and back again. Unseen currents hummed, reaching deep into the marrow of bones, yet uplifting, calling upon all those present to believe in the event about to begin: sea-nomad-becoming, the foremost rite of their tribe.

The shahiroh scrambled aboard, calling the seven candidates after them, guiding each to a separate bench, isolated from their companions.

Seaward, the sky was pale aquamarine torn with pink-tinted clouds. A marine bird screamed harshly. The Shahee began to heave at the canoe, which slid slowly out into the morning surf. This was a sight Kreh-ursh had often seen in the dawn, but always from the beach: sailors wading waist deep into the waves, spray cascading, drenching backs, shattering itself against the wooden hull.

At another command, the Shahee scrambled aboard, and paddles were grabbed up with bangs and rattles. There was a sharp smack as fifty blades hit the water in unison. The heavy canoe reared against the breakers, straining for the open sea. Soon they were sliding between rocky headlands, leaving the enclosed harbor behind. As the canoe struggled to the top of the first long ocean swell, Kreh-ursh could not resist sending a silent farewell to his village, to his parents and friends... but especially to that woman alone on the shingle. The horizon, paling to celestial blue, was now glimmering white-gold, echoed by the rolling banks of kree-eh that sucked in the growing light, reflecting it back through the waves. Then a bright sliver of the sun's disk slipped above the edge of the world. The great canoe, paddles flashing like fins, surged across the sea toward the sunrise.

5.
RENA

B een looking for you, Weasel!" As Jade jumped up to run, Rena dropped her board, and her weight crashed into Jade like a toppling tower of bricks. Jade struggled, yet the older girl had her, twisting an arm behind her back. Jade shrieked in pain.

"Come on, Weasel. Let's go and have a talk back there in the dunes. Uufghh!" Kyle had swung his boogie board at her back.

"Stop it, bully!" He was hysterical, his voice high-pitched with fear.

"It's okay, Kyle. We're just playing." The things you say. Rena ignored him then. Twisting Jade's other arm behind her, she frog-marched her up the sand. Jade knew she was done for. The best she could hope would be to end up like Miguel, with a broken arm or worse. What an idiot! Why get on the unsociable side of someone with three times your killing power? If only she could teleport, find herself on a different planet. But they were closing on the dunes. She was in serious trouble. Teleporting did not exist. Soon Jade would not exist either. Kyle's dumb screaming in her ears would be the final thing she ever heard.

Then a piercing whistle ripped through the summer's day, knocking a couple of surfers off their boards. For once, Jade felt relief—the one person around here who could roast and spit Rena as easy as look at her. The older girl let go of her arms, throwing her down. She spat out:

"So you had to bring your mom with you for protection, did you? Well, stay scared, Weasel. I'll get you soon. And it'll be worse than when I took care of your South American buddy."

Jade, rubbing her arms, couldn't resist: "I'm sure you will: you and your mates. That was so brave, what you did to Miguel—three of you against one guy half your size."

Rena walked back and picked up her board. She turned and smiled at Jade, but there was nothing friendly there. "Promise you, then, Weasel: when I deal with you, it'll be just you and me."

She looked for a moment at Jade's mother approaching down the beach. But the closer Joan got, the more Rena shrank into herself. She had lost her prey this time. Before Joan got anywhere near the spot where the three of them were standing, Rena turned on her heel and slouched away toward the other end of the beach. Jade realized she was shaking and sat down quickly to hide the fact. She stared at the sand, trying to pull herself together, remembering to say, while their mother was still well out of earshot:

"Kyle, one word to Mom about that, and you're history, okay?"

"Jade, you're always thinking I'm gonna go running to Mom. I'm not gonna say anything, but why is she after you? Have you done something wrong? Did you go up to the lab site? I bet you did, you and Darren and that Miggy-lorito zee-senyorrrito!"

Their mother was getting closer.

"What'll you give me if I don't tell Mom? Jaa-ade… girls who are grounded aren't allowed to go surfing…"

"Whatever, you can use my bike… for a week."

"A month."

"Two weeks."

"Hi, Mom!"

"Okay, a month!"

Joan dropped her things on the beach beside them. "Was that girl one of your friends? She looked a little rough."

But Jade was already up and running for the waves, board under her arm, relief sending a rush of adrenalin through her body. While their mum was cool on many fronts, some things you just didn't tell parents.

Kyle came charging into the surf behind her, holding his boogie board out in front. He tripped as he hit the water and fell flat on his face in the shallows. Jade laughed. His board was way too big for him, and he had no idea how to handle it, but anything Jade had, Kyle wanted. He had whined and whined until their mother bought him a board. She headed out into the waves, her brother in tow.

The feel of the dragging water around her was refreshing as she paddled out. She loved the exhilaration, sun hot on her back as she rode her board up a wave and crashed through the fringe of foam at its crest, falling down the other side and heading on to the next.

It was only as she was paddling furiously in, building up speed to surf that first good wave at just the right point, that her attention was caught by something in the silver-blue slope down which she slid… Something flashed and the world went black… She was careering down a dark glass funnel into the ocean's entrails… the wave racing faster, curling tighter, tighter still... A boy's laughter echoed as the universe groaned and swallowed her whole.

6.
THE RIFT

Taashou entered the sandy cave, leaning on Lehd. Every year the mountain cost her more; this year had been the worst. She longed for a relaxing soak in the mineral baths of the community, but that could come later. There was work to be done.

"Who saw the rift? How do you know? You were with me up on Kaa-meer-geh. You saw how quiet the mountain was."

Yet before Lehd could answer, another voice spoke up:

"It hasn't come through the mountain, but it is definitely the rift."

Out of the cluster of shahiroh standing in the cave's center stepped the man who had spoken. He was older than Taashou yet stood straight and fit despite a certain haggardness of features. His only clothing was a tight-fitting suit made of brown kelp. It even reached up into a hood that melded seamlessly into the skin of his face. He wore gloves and boots that extended into stiff, finlike appendages.

"Daakohn." She smiled despite her weariness. "Daakohn-bhah-ehl-bhah-her, you are the only person who could make such a claim and have me believe it. I'm glad you are back."

"I won't stay. My mount misses me already, but it's good to see you, Taashou."

"So the rift? But how? If not through the mountain, for what purpose have we been camping on this barren lump of rock for so long? Kaa-meer-geh was the point of melding."

"This time it has come through the sea."

"It cannot be the same!"

"Taashou, no living person on this world knows it as I do. Every molecule in my body shrieks at the recognition. It is the same for my mount."

Taashou looked around at the bare cave that was their home, had been since Daakohn had come back to them all those years ago. Openings around the walls led to rudimentary sleeping chambers and storerooms, with torches and blubber oil lamps for lighting. For meetings and meals they stood or sat on mats in this wide space. But that was it. The red mountain offered little more.

"So how?"

He shrugged.

"I know only that the rift has reappeared. This time it has come as a sort of tunnel through the sea, or whirlpool."

"A whirlpool? I wonder if that will be any more tolerable than through fire?"

"It is the worst experience any living creature could bear. Fire or water, nothing in this world prepares you."

"Prepare… if we could. We cannot even know…"

"It explains the imbalance we have felt in the ocean all this spring."

The newest speaker was also one of the shahiroh, clad like Taashou in blue, yet twenty years or so her junior. "We have felt the pull, but it was just a strangeness. We could not define it…"

"That could not be," Taashou answered the man. "There is a natural equilibrium that establishes when the rift opens. Your strangeness comes from another source."

"I agree with Bel-geer," said Daakohn, "I too have felt it… a lessening of life, or of the life force. It is pulling strongly at Shah. Taashou, I was seventeen when I experienced the rift and knew nothing of its nature. Yet I who then was the youngest am now the oldest, and I feel that this time it is different."

"Have you located the region?"

"Somewhere about two to four days northwest of the Sacred Isle—with a good wind."

Taashou was silent for a moment. Then she spoke:

"Seven of our young people have just been summoned to their initiation. We must protect them during their ordeal. Once sea-nomad-becoming has finished, we will turn our attention to this."

"That may be too late," Daakohn warned.

"I have made my decision."

"We may not have such a luxury of time as you imagine."

"It is the risk I take."

"The risk all of us bear."

7.
100% EFFICIENT! NO EMISSIONS!

Jade was hurled and bumped upside down, head over heels, every which way, sand and salt in eyes, ears, mouth, and nose. Finally, she was scraped, rolled, and washed into the frothing shallows, buckets of sand filling her shorts, a gallon of sea water down her throat. She could have, should have, handled that wave effortlessly. She got up warily, checking to see who might have seen her get dunked by such an easy wave. Rena was now down the other end of the beach with the older surfers. This time at least she had been spared.

It was that vision of a watery abyss that had overcome her, spiraling down into the horrific dark... a sort of waking nightmare. She knew it had something to do with her dream on the beach, and with that colored algae that had slopped into the water around her from Rena's launch. A kind of whirlpool, only faster, darker... and that groaning. It had been triggered by colors. She had seen a brightly colored spot on the beach: her mom, wearing that ridiculous swimsuit, looking like an unfinished Rubik's cube somebody gave up on.

She looked out to sea. That was when she noticed the clouds. Like no weather pattern she had ever seen. The entire sky was swirling around, as if some huge basin of cloudy liquid had just had the plug pulled and was spiraling down the drain. Except that this was upside down, and those clouds looked like they were being sucked up into the sky. Below them, on the horizon, the three towers of the experimental biofuel station almost seemed to center and anchor the billowing formation over their particular patch of sea.

Farther in, she caught a flash of bright orange. Kyle was paddling into the path of a huge wave that threatened to eat him whole. He turned his board just at the wrong time, valiantly attempting to catch it. The wave towered high above, menacing and immobile. Then it came crashing down, an avalanche of foam under which he disappeared. His orange boogie board shot vertically up out of the water like a rocket from a submarine launcher. A few seconds later, his body tumbled up onto the beach in a swirl of surf. Well, at least she was not the worst surfer out that day. She called to him:

"Kyle, I'm going inshore!"

"I'm not. There's a whole pile on their way. Look."

"Nah. Those are tiny. Don't go out beyond your

depth, okay?"

Jade waded in, ran up the beach, and threw herself down on her towel. Now she could see her mom's horrendous swimsuit up close.

Joan beamed: "Do you like it?"

It was the grossest thing Jade had ever seen. Radioactive green. Purple and orange lizards, or alligators—she could not tell which—swarmed across it. Every second animal was wearing a bright yellow sunhat, or holding a bunch of pink flowers. Just looking at it brought on her queasiness. She looked away.

"Yeah, it's nice, Mom. We can tell the lighthouse keeper on Point Mauri he's out of a job. We'll just get you to stand up there every night and shine a torch on you."

Joan hit her with her red and purple floppy sunhat, frowning mock angrily: "Such a charming girl I've raised!"

Jade closed her eyes and lay back, then giggled: "You could even double as an outdoor disco. Only thing missing are the strobe lights!"

Her mother ignored her: "This'll interest you. We're in the news!"

Jade sat up and watched the newscast on her mom's phone.

"MAURI COVE LAUNCHES ECO-FUEL," rolled the headline over video images of Mauri Cove and surrounding coastline as a commentary droned, "Last night, quiet Mauri Cove took a giant step toward the development of an ecologically harmonious society when Synengine Energies launched its new synthetic fuels laboratory. Synengine Energies is a multinational group with installations in over fifteen countries."

The picture snapped to Mayor Robbins' rosy face: "Their choice of our town as a base for this experimental facility is a great boost for local employment. We must support this bid for a clean, green future in this wonderful region."

Then a harder visage appeared, cloaked in dark glasses, under which Jade read, "Dr. Norman Hagues, CEO, Synengine Energies Inc." His voice sounded like gravel under car tires: "We are proud to be collaborating with the people of this town to create more jobs... a better future for your kids in a more loving, trusting world..."

"The new fuel is 100% efficient, producing no emissions," the newscaster's voice continued. "Furthermore, the refinement process creates absolutely no waste..."

The screen changed to a shot of a crystal flask containing an oily substance that danced and flowed in sparkling colors. Jade gasped as a deja-vu feeling thumped her in her guts. She tried to shake it: "Wow. They open a science lab here, and that makes us superstars!"

She lay back on her towel, closing her eyes. Her mind drifted back to that tunnel... It was all fading... the sun leaching out her strength. It didn't matter.

"Jade! What's that?"

Sitting up, she saw her mom squinting down at the water. The sun shining off the surface meant that all she could see was the sea's green-gold glitter.

"What?" As her eyes adjusted, she discerned her brother having another go at riding a wave. Kyle was not paddling out far enough to catch them before they broke. Then he'd sit on his board waiting too long. The truth was his arms were way too short for him to get up a decent speed. She chuckled.

"Look!"

She looked. "All I see is one really bad surfer. You know, Kyle just doesn't have what it takes in the surfing department."

"You weren't so hot yourself when you were his age, Miss Superior. But I don't mean Kyle. What's that out there?"

Now that her eyes had got used to the glare, Jade saw, beyond the breakers, what looked like a dark smudge on the water. It was moving, but not very fast. Could it be a school of fish? Or a… It didn't look like any creature she recognized. The long, dark shape slid slowly, calmly, across the bay. Her mother's voice was tense but calm:

"Come on, let's get Kyle out of the water."

8.
ALONE

The sky was aflame with gold, ruby red, and polished copper. Streaks of purple like the shreds of a king's robe snagged the clouds, as if some titan-sized monarch, fleeing for his life, had left his riches strewn across the battlefield of his defeat. The endless sea reflected the sunset's colors, and as hard as he scanned the horizon line, Kreh-ursh could see no break or cloud to indicate the land where his people's village lay nestled in its protected bay.

His body still rolled from the waves' motion. Even here on the sand, he could sense the bottomless deep of the ocean below, hear whispering currents flowing all around. The solid shore pitched and dipped as if this island too were an enormous vessel, a thousand times larger, a million times older than the great canoe that had dropped him here just a short time ago.

The landing was abrupt. That morning Kreh-ursh had watched the twin bluffs that harbored his home meld into the line of the coast. Eventually, even that verdant band had sunk below the horizon without a final farewell. Then only waves remained, heaving the canoe high, releasing it into their troughs.

At that point the shahiroh had blindfolded him, depriving him of any chance to track their course. Soon he felt the canoe change direction. Though he tried to chart their course from the prevailing breeze and slap of waves against the hull, the regular stroke of the Shahees' paddles put him off. Finally he gave up. They were heading generally east. He would have to plot his position afresh when they arrived. So he sat, blind and silent, allowing the ocean's green music to soften the pain of leaving home, and seduce him with its whispered promises of adventure. Throughout the day they traveled, the Shahees' paddles slicing a regular rhythm under a relentless sun.

As they approached Zjhuud-geh, sighted late in the afternoon, with the sun sinking behind them, his blindfold was removed. Squinting, Kreh-ursh glanced back at Geh-meer, but she looked totally absorbed in herself. Then his attention was grabbed by the island as they skirted its reef in a wide circle. Huge rollers ripped themselves to silvery ribbons on its perimeter.

Finally, the chief shahiroh called out a command, and the vessel turned and began to surf in on the back of a slow roller. A low hum arose fore and aft, resonating through the craft's timbers, issuing from the mouths of Shahee and shahiroh. The entire vessel began to tingle, raising goose bumps up and down Kreh-ursh's arms. All the Shahee strained their paddles into the water with more force than ever, pushing the great canoe ever harder and faster, straight toward the island. Just as it looked like they would be dashed into pieces against the coral—marked by a line of crashing surf ahead—all seven shahiroh rose to their feet with a belly-rich shout. Their gray-blue robes flapped and snapped like ragged wings in the wind. Surf flashed, wrapping the canoe in silver mist. It seemed to Kreh-ursh that the fine vapor acted as a kind of cushion, lifting and carrying the heavy vessel over the sharp coral. Then they were sliding through into the smooth waters of the lagoon, the violence of the ocean behind them.

A deep calm surrounded the voyagers. The air was heavy, as if it had lain undisturbed for long years. Yet the ocean's fresh salt still laced the atmosphere. Barely a breeze blew to disturb the evening's warmth, the sun stretching its seductive rays over the island's shoulder. A sense of peacefulness pervaded after their day-long battle against the currents. Unknown perfumes wafted across the lagoon, underscored by the warm wetness of rotting plant life. After a day away from land, the smell felt like a welcome.

Zjhuud-geh was an ancient volcano. Perfectly round, its steep cone seemed to touch the sky. Lava flows, forgotten in prehistory, had scored deep valleys down its slopes and carved rocky bays and inlets out of its coastline. Except for the bare peak, trailing its wisp of smoke, it was covered in dense jungle, which even spilled out onto the crescent-shaped, golden beaches, creating an impenetrable curtain between land and sea.

They circled the island to the gentle sound of waves softly washing sand, slapping rock above the reef's dull roar. That and the rhythmic dip of paddles, kept in time by the chief shahiroh's clicking tongue. From the island came the thousand-throated rustling of living jungle—tweets, calls, shrieks, and whistles pricking the continuous noise like golden embroidery on a vast emerald tapestry.

Finally, the canoe glided into this protected bay. When its keel gently bumped aground, the chief shahiroh approached Kreh-ursh, sitting farthest forward in the canoe. She jerked her thumb at the beach and growled a brief command. He scrambled over the side into thigh-deep water and stood watching as his only contact with home backed slowly out of the bay, turned, and slid out of sight around a rocky headland.

Now he gazed at the sunset. A feeling of loneliness and desolation washed over him like a slow, glassy wave—huge, green, and cold. As the fiery colors of the sun gave way to twilit purples, a cool breeze flowed across the water. Thinking about a fire and a place to sleep, he walked off along the shore, looking for driftwood.

9.
RESCUE

Joan had jumped up and was running toward the water's edge, her daughter powering after. Jade overtook her on the hard sand near the water and went crashing into the surf, yelling, "Kyle! Kyle! Come in!"

But in the brief moments they had taken their eyes off him, her brother had managed to get a long way out, surprisingly so. His tiny figure on the bright orange board flipped quite expertly over an incoming wave. He must have worked out that he was taking the waves too near the beach, but he was now too far to surf a wave back in. He was near the swift ocean current that flowed past the heads. Jade could no longer see any dark shape in the water. In any case, it had looked much too big for a shark, hadn't it? How big did sharks grow? Some other fish? A killer whale?

She realized her board was up the beach next to their towels. No time to run back. Her mother crashed into the surf beside her.

"Stay here!" Joan commanded, her lawyer voice one you did not disobey. Yet she hesitated, looking along the sand. All the other swimmers were far down the other end. She waded deeper, calling to Kyle, but the distant figure seemed not to hear. Jade knew her mother was not such a great swimmer.

"No, Mom. You stay, I'll go."

Without waiting for an answer, Jade plunged in and began to swim out with powerful strokes. She tried to keep her mind off the dark shape, not to think about the pair of enormous jaws with jagged, shining teeth that might close around her legs, pull her down. She couldn't imagine how painful a shark bite might be, whether the teeth sliced straight through or needed two or three good chomps to sever a thigh muscle. Maybe it was so quick, you didn't feel it. Or maybe… Her fear energized her as never before. Don't think, just swim, get out to Kyle. Three years of classes — before the summer she had passed the second level of her First Aid and Life Saving Certificate—meant she was a good enough swimmer. When a wave came at her, she dived under, then popped up the other side. Every couple of minutes she tried to sight Kyle and adjust her course. No sign of the dark shape. That was good news, she hoped.

Soon she was within fifty yards of him, a fragile waif on a vast, undulating field of green. Looking tired and miserable, he was sitting on his board crying, having realized he could not reach the shore again, with no strength left to paddle. Seeing Jade, his eyes lit up.

"No!" Jade yelled.

But he had already thrown himself from his board and begun thrashing through the peaking waves. It was the worst thing he could do.

"Stay with your board!"

Kyle did not seem to hear. If he reached Jade and tried to grab her, he might pull them both under. Jade looked around, could see no sign of any big fish. Kyle was still over thirty yards away when suddenly he yelped, plunging under the water. Jade cried out, launching herself toward her brother. Yet when he burst up again to the surface, he was not ripped in two; no bright blood foamed red into the green; there was no gory, shark-inflicted wound as Jade had imagined, no flashing teeth. Instead, he was plastered in thick, brown goo that had coated his skin and hair. It formed a greasy mat extending all around him. Like oil or grease, it floated in a long, rolling raft on the surface, weighing him down. He went under again. Jade moved closer, doing the breast stroke, but was unsure how to act. If she tried to reach him, she would also get trapped. Maybe she would not be able to keep herself afloat, let alone Kyle. She circled around where he was struggling.

"Swim toward me!" she called. "Get yourself out of it!"

Her brother was also a good swimmer for his age, but Jade could see he was getting seriously tired. She had to act. Just as she was about to plunge forward, a flash against the green made her turn her head: Kyle's orange board slipping down the side of a wave. She swam over and grabbed it. Then she closed to where her brother was struggling. Giant waves heaved them up and down, but the slick hugged the surface like a heavy blanket.

"Kyle! Grab on!"

Jade pushed the board toward him, opening up a channel through the ooze. Though Kyle scrabbled wildly, his oily hands slipped, unable to gain a proper grip. Some of the scum wrapped around Jade's shoulders and arms as well. It felt heavy, dragging her down—strange, the way it floated. Finally, Kyle was able to heave his body half onto the board. Jade kicked backward, hard. The muck was closing in. More of it stuck to her body, staining her limbs. She kept kicking as hard as she could, struggling to keep her head free.

Then they were clear, heading for the beach. But that golden strip appeared a lifetime away, visible like paradise in distant glimpses between the moving hills. They had drifted a long way out. The same wind that had pulled Kyle so far had blown them both over half a mile out, far beyond Point Mauri. Below her, Jade felt the strong pull of the ocean current sliding sideways down the coast and out again to sea. How would they escape?

She made sure Kyle was lying securely. He was retching and coughing but conscious. Then she began to swim slowly shoreward. It was not easy. She had to pull the board, swimming with only one arm, unable to get behind to kick because the lower half of Kyle's body hung down into the sea. She kept pulling, thrashing along with one arm, kicking as hard as she could, but the coast was not getting any closer. She must not give up. She knew about swimming across the current to escape from the rip, but it took all the strength she could muster. A large wave broke unexpectedly over them. Jade swallowed water and lost her stroke. She rested for a few moments, trying to cough the seawater from her lungs and get her bearings. Then she kept going. Soon she swallowed more water. This time she did not stop, could not. Her vision was beginning to blur. She could no longer tell whether she was still swimming in the direction of the coast or not, but forced herself to continue, not fighting the current, just trying to cross it. They must have been swept far down the coast by now. Her swimming arm had now become a dead weight from tiredness. She grabbed the board with that hand and began to use the other to swim with. It was her weakest arm. Kyle started to slide off the board. Jade had no more strength.

"Hold on, Kyle! You must hold on!"

He stirred, seemed to hear his sister. Though he did not pull himself back onto the board, he gripped harder. Jade became aware of a buzzing sound in her ears, getting steadily louder. This was what happened before you passed out. She must not! Yet still the buzzing got stronger. She resisted, struck out harder with arm and legs. The buzzing became a consistent, slapping drone. It seemed to be more intense with each wave she pushed through. She knew she was just hallucinating because she was getting tired, had no idea whether the beach was any closer. If only she could see it! Maybe she was just swimming in circles.

Then over the top of a wave she glimpsed an aluminum hull, a small dinghy. The drone became the roar of an outboard, and a boat came alongside. Strong, adult hands were pulling Kyle up out of the water. With the movement, the metal hull swung toward her and smacked against her head. The shock left her gasping, breathing in water. She realized she had made a bad mistake… she couldn't breathe! Couldn't see! A fogginess enwrapped her and she began to sink into the deep green. Then a firm hand grabbed her abruptly, vice-like, under the arm. It hauled at her, pulling her toward the surface. Her head whacked the metal side again. Then she was being raised from water into air—pure, rich, clean air! But her lungs were drowned and she still could not breathe. The haze turned black, like night. The last thing she felt was her head painfully crack a third time, against the floor of the boat as she was laid down. Then everything switched off.

10.
TRANCE

Bronze tongues of flame flickered hungrily up toward the six meer-zjhur, or redfish, dangling from a sharpened stick above the fire. The smell of roasting flesh stabbed at Kreh-ursh's stomach. He had drunk more of his potion than he knew he should. If things went well, he would have to survive on this island for at least twenty days, maybe longer. He must not waste the potion. In the canoe he had tried to be as firm as possible, but by mid-morning the rumbling in his stomach must have been audible to the entire crew. At noon, when the paddlers ceased their stroke to eat a scanty meal of dried fish and vegetables, he limited himself to a few sips. Then he fixed his concentration on an invisible point in his mind and tried to shut out the obscenely loud sounds of chewing, belching, and swallowing. In the afternoon, his stomach seemed to shrink, happily, and he did not much notice his hunger.

Now, though, the pain was like a dagger, lacerating his insides, demanding food. He could smell it all around. Apart from fish and other seafood that must inhabit the waters of the bay in abundance, his oversensitive nostrils seduced him with the perfume of tropical fruit. He could smell maa-sheesh, the plump, fist-sized fruit with flesh the color of ocean surf and a taste of both sugar and salt that grew on the lowlands around the coast. The wind also brought the scent of baal-aarsh melons, which looked like volcanic rocks on the outside but were the most intense sunset orange within. They were chewy, tangy, full of juice, and his mouth watered at the thought of them. Then the wind briefly changed, and he was sure he could faintly detect, wafted down from the volcano's higher slopes, the sugary-acid bite of the bluish purple zjheh-rohsh clusters, lounging on their low vines among the trees.

He finally pulled a fish impatiently from the skewer. It was agony to chew slowly and carefully, locating the many spines with his tongue and spitting them into the fire, when what he really wanted to do was wolf the flesh down as fast as he could. He managed to curb his hunger, finishing off just three of the fish. Those that remained, he wrapped in a large leaf to save for the next day. Sea-nomad-becoming required continual exertion. He had only the potion prepared by his mother and food he had time to gather. He needed to ration himself.

Then, huddling close to the little fire in its hearth of sand, he stared into the flames, clearing his mind to begin the exercises. His eyes searched through the embers, seeking the different colors he could find there, relaxing, tuning his concentration, emptying his mind of thought. The flames absorbed his complete attention. Little by little he began to see beyond...

The shahiroh appeared with no warning, but not suddenly. She seemed to materialize out of the firelight on the far side of the fire. When he became aware of her, Kreh-ursh was unsure how long she had been standing there. She gave the impression of having existed since the birth of time, growing from the sand like an ancient, black-rooted loman tree. Her dark robes merged with the darkness behind her, the ceremonial mask could be a gray-silver billow of smoke frozen perversely in its horrible grimace, and her power enwrapped her like an invisible cloak. Behind the carved wood only the shining points of her eyes—glittering jewels that anchored her in time and space—and the harsh rasp of her breath through the breathing hole showed she was alive.

Immersed as he was in trance, he did not jump up or make any outward movement. Yet his mind tensed, on guard. The shahiroh, more knowledgeable in lore and craft than the other villagers, were unpredictable and dangerous. They observed each other for long moments. He felt her probing subtly at his mind. Then she mind-spoke:

Kreh-ursh, I am glad to be your mentor for sea-nomad-becoming.

So articulate was her mind speech, so accurate, it was almost as if she were speaking directly to him in words. And her friendly tone disarmed him.

Hoh-ee, Taashou.

He recognized her despite her mask, this lean,

haughty woman he had known all his life. They said she undertook sea-nomad-becoming at twelve years old, the youngest candidate the village had ever known. Her name meant "waving grass spear."

She now reached under her robes, brought forth her clenched fist. In a scattering movement, she tossed fine green powder into the fire. It erupted. Flames leaped. Thick green-gray smoke seethed out, the fumes clogging his throat. Heat singed his cheeks. His eyes watered. He coughed, but the smoke was already swirling thickly inside his head. His inner sight bucked and rolled, wild and unstable. Taashou's presence was there, before him, demanding. Her eyes, two obsidian chunks, locked onto his own. All he could see were those points burrowing deep, forcing him to hold her gaze. He stared through the flames. Beyond the shining came the visions…

Tell me. Describe what you see.

There's a jungle… rainforest… I'm walking… thick forest…

Vines and creepers fell around him, hung above. The sun's rays reached down through high trunks, but they produced a green, underwater light.

…looking for…

He examined the trees. He was searching for something. Here were trees as wide as two or three men lying end to end, as tall as the great canoe placed upright, even taller. Yet he was not looking for these. He had to find a single trunk, the one right for him, the one that would be his own. He walked through trees, trees and trees, vaguely tracing a large circle, keeping the upslope of the volcano on his right—for he was in the forest on Zjhuud-geh. Suddenly he saw it —his tree—a taat-eh trunk about his own age. It was slim and straight, its branches not spreading from the trunk until high above his head, possibly two, three times his own height. He knew it was the one he should select. Mentally, he tried to mark its position.

Explain.

I have found my tree.

Continue.

The scene shifted, and he was skimming across ocean waves, clipping white tops in a brisk breeze. Then he dived into the depths:

Underwater... Shah, the sea...

Green sunlight slanted through the waves in sharp bars. Then all kinds of sea life was writhing nearby: shoals of the ever-present kree-eh refracting every rainbow color through the translucent water; groups of lilac rruush-oh billowing dreamily; a sinuous Shah-skur rolling its beige and cream coils along the sandy bottom; even a majestic taa-zjhur gliding along, its purple and gold hide flashing in the sunlight. He showed all this to Taashou.

All at once the marine life disappeared. Cloud covered the scene, and he was again on the surface, but now it was calm. The water felt hard and heavy like molten metal.

Describe.

It is... No... It can't be...

Describe.

He was looking down into the water. It was not possible. Trance during initiation gifted visions of possible future pathways, yet this was unreal. If he was seeing what he thought he saw, it could no longer be a glimpse into his own future or any other reality, but a creature from the realm of pure myth.

II.
PLAYING THE HERO?

Jade was feeling fragile despite Dr. Bilges having given her the all-clear. She must have been out for a bare few minutes, because when she came to—vomiting over the gunwale—even though the pot-bellied old fisherman in the stern was nearly shaking his tiny outboard off its mountings, they were still a good five hundred yards from the beach. Her mother had her arms tightly around her waist, squeezing her, making her vomit up all the water she had swallowed. She spent the rest of the journey to the beach coughing herself stupid and puking over the side while Joan went and held Kyle. Her brother had barely been conscious when they pulled him into the boat. Face, limbs, and body were plastered with the dark sludge, the color of a bruise. Added to that, the smell of it was revolting: a strange blend of rotting things and vinegar... and something else, like turpentine. Kyle was trembling and shaking, seeming to get continuously weaker in Joan's arms.

Jade saw all this in glimpses every time she raised

her head. Her nausea was back in force. She felt as if she were reliving her dream. Blotches of red, blue, orange, yellow, pink, and white exploded before her eyes, and a black mist hovered at the edges of her vision, threatening to drag her down again into unconsciousness. Through the haze, she noticed her mother's cell phone lying in a puddle of water in the bottom of the boat, as if she had dropped it in the middle of a conversation to do something else. Jade picked it up, but the screen was dead.

As they neared the shore, the old fisherman aimed his boat straight at the beach. Through luck, or experience, he managed to catch a perfect wave, and they surfed in with a speed and skill that Jade had to admire. As the aluminum hull rasped onto the concrete boat ramp, Patrick—Jade and Kyle's stepfather—was there, reaching over the side. He scooped Kyle up in one swift movement and began running up the beach, yelling over his shoulder at Joan to help Jade. A small crowd had gathered and were staring at them as if they were aliens come down from a distant planet. Rena and her mates, Screwdriver and the Head, were standing off to one side.

"What happened, Weasel? Go out over your depth? Oughta remember to wear your water-wings next time."

Jerks! Jade thought, but she needed all her strength to keep walking, supported by her mother and the fisherman.

Joan paused, however, and said, "What's your problem? My daughter has just saved her brother's life. While you, when it came to the crunch, for all your puff and big words, were about as much use as an origami manual on a building site."

Rena stopped smiling. She turned and stomped off down the beach, her two cronies in tow.

Patrick's car was parked, or rather ploughed into the soft sand, beside the boat ramp. For one long moment she doubted they would get free. The wheels spun and spat sand before they gripped and revved back onto firm tarmac. It took them less than five minutes to reach Dr. Bilges' surgery, just a couple of rooms built onto the side of his house near the village center. Jade and Kyle had been coming here since they were tiny, so the flagstone path down past the rose garden brought back every childhood misadventure. Mrs. Cotild, the nurse—generously built, generous with sweets when they were good, but with her tongue when they were not—opened the door.

"Lordy! What happened to the poor laddie? Get him in here quick. Come on, bring him straight through."

Patrick laid Kyle onto the examination table in the surgery.

Jade was shunted onto a chair in the corner. Bilges blew his metallic, disinfectant breath across her.

"Let's have a look. Been playing the heroine again, have you?"

"No, I just…"

"Drink this down—in one. That's it."

The milky liquid tasted of chalk. Mrs. Cotild laid a hand on her shoulder.

"Right, come along with me, lassie. We haven't finished with you yet."

She followed the nurse through a door into the doctor's house, along a hall to his bathroom.

"Don't go scraping any of that goo onto the doctor's walls, hear me? Okay, kit off and under that shower."

Jade scrubbed at her body, using a vomit-smelling soap Mrs. Cotild had left her. The sludge stained her arms, legs, even her neck. Even after she managed to scrape off the rubbery substance, which coagulated in the plughole, her skin was left discolored by a repugnant tinge. When she returned, dressed in shorts and a sweater of the doctor's, Mrs. Cotild thrust a cup of hot soup into her hands and wrapped her in a blanket.

"Get that down you and see if you can't get a bit of rest, lass, until we finish with your brother."

Bilges had some sort of tube sticking in Kyle's nose while he lay on his side on the examination table. Joan and Patrick stood woodenly in the center of the small room, each peering over one of the doctor's shoulders. Mrs. Cotild had squeezed her bulk between the filing cabinet and the examination table, and was wiping Kyle's tears away. It felt like a scene from *ER* except Jade had no idea it all felt quite so horrible when it actually happened. Deep down in her gut she felt hideous. Everyone looked pale and worried. For the first time, she had to accept, to realize the consequences of what she was responsible for: This was her doing. It was all her fault for leaving her brother alone in the water.

No, Kyle would be okay as long as he could throw up everything he swallowed in the sea. He would recover. Any minute now, it would be over. They could go back home and have dinner, watch television, do everything they always did in the evenings. Tomorrow they could go to the beach again. She would look after him better this time, not go and lie on her towel while he was out there, not even if their mom was watching, too. If she had stayed in the water with Kyle, she might have kept him from heading so far out. The weird thing was that Dr. Bilges, Mrs. Cotild, everybody kept calling her a heroine—even Patrick had said it—yet it was her fault that Kyle was lying here crying with a tube sticking up his nose.

She closed her eyes, tried to relax.

"Jade! Are you okay? Feeling all right?"

Her eyes snapped open at Patrick's voice. She had drifted off. Patrick put his arm around her. "Time for us to hit the road."

They thanked the doctor and trailed out to the car. As they drove home, Jade thought about the slick. It was still floating around out there, but where had it come from?

After leaving town by the motorway that ran down the coast, just over the bridge from the turnoff to their beach, they drove by a place where the countryside was scarred by a wide swath of graded earth. This was the site of Jade's troubles with Rena. The Synengine research facility: a squat, white concrete block, harsh against the green fields and darker forest across the river. Two aluminum chimneys rose ten yards high, gleaming in late sunlight. From the right-hand funnel a wisp of pale smoke or steam drifted, but otherwise there was no movement. In the car park, a dozen or so workers' cars sat beside a flash, lead-colored BMW belonging to the Synengine CEO, Dr. Hagues.

"That place is so ugly!"

From the front seat, Joan raised her head from nursing Kyle: "It's for a good cause. Sometimes we have to accept a little ugliness in life to help improve the world."

"I'll never accept an ugly life."

They skirted the perimeter and turned onto Point Mauri Road, leaving the looming monstrosity behind. Then they were traveling between fields on the right and the Mauri River on their left. On the far shore, gloomy in twilight, rose the native forest reserve, a dark, closed mass of vegetation. The road curved, and dunes came between them and the river mouth, hiding the sea, which lay east. Finally, they turned right, into their own road, and roared up their driveway.

Later, lying in bed—after having eaten some hot stew Patrick had cooked up—Jade's queasiness returned. This time it didn't strike as strongly as before, yet seemed to creep into her consciousness quietly—as a sort of waking dream. All those competing colors whirled about in her head, and sounds of the sea seemed to follow her heartbeat softly, insistently. Something wanted to be acknowledged. She could hear a mocking voice, the boy's, and a trace of his laugh. He seemed to be forming words, yet she felt weak, could not understand the sounds... *hursshh... faa... daw... oh...* Little by little her concentration frayed, drifting away into the wide night. She slipped down into a silky, dreamless sleep.

12.
DEATH

A lake... *so large... it is Bhaanj-krraash-oh-bhaan...* Kreh-ursh felt bewildered. It must be... Dragon-Belly Lake... but why was this mythical place appearing in his vision? Purple-brown peaks rose jaggedly all around the broken sides of an ancient crater that formed the lakeshore. Sun flashed into his eyes off the water's flat surface. His disembodied awareness hovered above, staring down into the still depths.

Describe...

Nothing. Dead. Still...

Then he saw it, could hardly believe his eyes: a creature he had only ever heard of in stories...

Here... it can't be...

Why was it entering his vision? His eyes were dazzled by the bright, changing colors. He had to be mistaken, but no underwater creature could come close to this for such awe-inspiring beauty. It really was...

Describe.

Ee... ee-kawg-zjhur!!!

Ee-kawg-zjhur... the mythical jewel fish. Almost as

soon as he spied it, the fish flipped out of his sight. With that, the vision dissolved, giving him no time to react or reflect on what he had seen.

Smoke swirled, wafting him deeper into its billows. As it cleared, in the fire's heart, a scene was forming: He was standing inside a bright, white-lit building. A young boy lay on a high bed, such as the Rraawuu city dwellers used inland. He was pale with sickness. People—probably the boy's family—stood around, dressed in peculiar, clinging garments.

Then that scene dissolved. He was carried across plains. Cloud shadows chased each other over waves of grass forever rippling like a wind-blown sea. A silver mist approached from the horizon. He was intrigued, the way it undulated, changing and flowing… Then the silver took substance, the earth trembled underfoot. He realized he was watching a huge herd of white and gray beasts thundering wildly through the knee-high grasses. They galloped closer, and he identified flying manes, tails, snorting nostrils, and pounding hooves… He saw horns: thin, straight, gleaming ivory sprouting from each beast's forehead. Then they were upon him. The dust of their passing rose up, obscuring their forms. The blowing grass melded into the fire's green-gray smoke, and the vision flowed onwards, carrying him toward…

Kaa-meer-geh…

Why?

A… ritual… don't understand…

The secret island of the shahiroh. What did it mean? To see this, he must have to go there… but only the shahiroh, the sea callers, came onto this island. Yet it could be no other: Everything was red rock and dust, and that smoldering crater dominated the skyline. There was a wide, sandy space, surrounded by a ring of wooden stakes driven into the ground. Beyond, he saw huts similar to his own but somehow more brooding, more mysterious, and farther off, the mouths of caves. Groups of shahiroh stood in the central area, identified by their blue robes. They appeared to be chanting, but he heard nothing. One of the shahiroh approached a kneeling figure, hooded, in green, holding a clay cup of some liquid. And he knew that person…

But the scene had changed once more, and now he was flying high in the air. He glided up a steep green valley over which two volcano-like peaks towered. They gleamed silver in the sunlight.

Gehg… Mountains!

His thoughts were now flowing fluidly to Taashou, verbalized mentally even as he formulated them. The vision dragged him back:

…sun shining… freezing wind…

A wind that roared down the valley. The air was colder than he had ever felt in his life, and that chill whiteness covering them, which he had heard about but never seen before, that must be snow. That was why it was cold. One of the peaks was slightly higher than the other. Could they be Geh-urbh-geh-ot?

Heh… Taashou confirmed, *Geh-urbh-geh-ot.*

Big-brother-little-sister, the twin peaks at the center of the mainland, from which they say all creation sprang.

…high up, valley between two peaks… building… a building made of the sea!

At the top of the valley was a construction surrounded by

more snow. As shiny and translucent as the sea, yet it looked as hard as mountain stone, as if it were obsidian from the volcanoes, but clear not dark. Those parapets and turrets could not be real. It would be impossible to build such a palace. He drifted closer, distinguishing two frail figures standing before the building. They appeared old and stooped, a man and a woman. Then mist swirled again.

Now very dry… hot, scorching…

The vision had changed once more, showing him a dry desert, scorched and seared by heat. This was not like the desert he knew to the north, where low scrub and age-worn escarpments melded together in arid harmony. This dead dryness seemed to scream in the agony of its lifelessness, as if whatever growth it might once have had had been torn unnaturally from its back. In the middle was a trudging figure. A single line of footprints trailed away behind to the far horizon. Kreh-ursh glided closer on the wings of his trance. The figure stumbled, near death, parched with thirst. Then Kreh-ursh was almost alongside, and he was able to see that it was a young man, emaciated, only a few years older than himself. The skin of his face was burnt and parched, his clothes ragged and torn. The stranger raised his eyes—red, grit-filled — turning his face toward him… It could not be… It was himself! As the vision dissolved, his alter ego fell face forward in the sand and lay unmoving…

Describe.

…No!

He struggled with every scrap of willpower. Taashou did not insist. Then Kreh-ursh was fighting to be free of the oppressive smoke clouds that held him captive. He lashed out at Taashou with his mind. She did not strike back, but suddenly he was aware of the fire before him on the beach, the cold sand. The fire's smoke, normal and natural, swirled upwards into the night sky, and darkness eclipsed his inner sight.

He was exhausted. Abruptly aware of the long day, the lack of food, and his own emotional strain, he could not last any longer. Sagging, he noticed Taashou's arms around him, one hand massaging his temples, pressing insistently on a certain point. Then he was slipping toward sleep, wondering why Taashou had insisted on seeing into his visions… Is that normal? They were his own… secret… no other candidate had ever revealed… How many different scenes! Questions whirled in his brain, unresolved, but he was already entering a pleasantly dark, dreamless realm.

He did not see how Taashou caught him as he fell unconscious toward the fire, how she laid him gently on his sleeping mat within the fire's warmth and wrapped him in a blanket. Neither did he see, oblivious in his exhaustion, how she sat for a long time, gazing into the dying fire herself, another thousand unanswered questions flickering in her own dark eyes along with the firelight.

13.
CLOUDS

The next day Jade got up early. She went in to see Kyle before breakfast and found her mom there. Her brother was sitting up in bed, and Joan was helping him take some of Dr. Bilges' pills.

"They taste awful, Mom! Do I have to?"

"Come on, Kyle, they're to make you feel better. Just the three, and then you can have some breakfast."

He submitted silently, but immediately after he swallowed began to cough and retch, bringing the pills straight back up. "I can't, Mom. I don't want to go back to sleep. The bleeding man..."

"They won't put you to sleep. They're to stop your tummy hurting, dear. What bleeding man?"

"The man with the bleeding face. He came to save me, but he scares me."

"Can I do anything, Mom?"

Her mother was abrupt, tiredness and worry showing on her face:

"No! Sorry... Please, could you get us all some breakfast? That would be a help. Now, Kyle, stop talking nonsense and just take these pills, will you?"

She left them, Kyle now crying, his face a patchwork of red and brown blotches where tears and the sludge from the sea had stained his features. She remembered how he had looked as he began to slip down into that mass under the waves, and a stab of guilt shot through her.

Hoping to distract herself, she turned on the TV. It was a rerun of the earlier Mauri Cove item on the twenty-four-hour news channel her mom liked. And there onscreen was that flask of multicolored swirl. She froze the image. Was it possible? She was going crazy! But she could feel her frontal lobes beginning to pulse as if a headache were chasing her. That synthetic fuel… it was like her dream, like the swirls of seaweed that had surrounded her in the water. That's normal, she told herself. We always incorporate bits of reality into our dreams. Yet why should this substance she had never encountered before have such an effect on her?

An unexpected bright flash from outside drew her toward the window. It was a clear day, yet over the roofs of the line of houses that separated their home from Mauri Cove, a strange storm was brewing. Out to sea, beyond their bay, more clouds than before were stacked up like a huge frozen yogurt cone, yet darker, more sinister. They appeared to revolve in a slow whirl at least a mile wide. All around, the sun still shone… blue sky, summer heat.

Jade felt an uneasy dread grip her insides. Her face felt hot, yet her limbs were as cold and dead as clay. It was fear. She was too scared to move. But why? They were just clouds. All she could do was stand, gazing out at the summer's day and that ominous weather pattern. Another flash came, like lightning, from within the churning mass. She waited for more, but there was nothing. While she stood frozen at the window, staring at the sky, an odd thought drifted into her mind: *Help this boy... Save your brother...*

What boy? Her brother? She shook her head and stumbled from the window, but found herself staring into the television screen, at that image of sparkling, multicolor flakes suspended in that flask of biofuel. Panting, she looked around at their living room: settee, rugs, cushions, her mother's overdue library books piled on the coffee table...

It broke the spell. What was she thinking?! Breakfast... her mom wanted her to get them breakfast. She went into the kitchen. Patrick had beaten her to it. Waiting on the bench were three bowls of his homemade muesli with chopped fruit and yogurt. Jade grabbed a bowl like a life raft, a solid piece of reality she could grasp onto, to know what was real amid all this craziness. Concentrate on the small things, the normal things. She walked out onto the porch, sat down on its sun-drenched steps.

She kept her eyes on the concrete path, shrubs, trees, Patrick's car in the driveway. Each thing before her seemed to vibrate with some intense energy, as if all its molecules were vibrating, ready to burst out of the very structure that held it together. So the car could become a gas cloud or a tree, the concrete path could turn into a liquid pool before her eyes. Even herself—maybe she did not exist in a solid sense at all.

Perhaps she was just dust blown on the breeze? She tried to ignore that, had to, and began eating her breakfast, keeping her eyes fixed on the bowl... Yet it was as if Patrick had chopped ginger into it... Nausea threatened to overwhelm her... Red and yellow peaches seemed to palpitate viscerally against the soft brown wheat flakes and pale yogurt... The passionate purple of the berries began to throb like a heartbeat…

…hurzjh... faadaw... oh...

The sun turned black. She was among crashing waves again. Kyle screamed, trapped by the dark sludge... sucked under... downward. The ocean swirled, and he was drawn toward that whirlpool, a maelstrom of dark ooze. Scrabbling for his arms, she felt him slip... begin to sink... Jade was screaming, "Hold on, Kyle! You must hold on!" yet Kyle's greasy fingers slithered from her own, and the current sucked him away… The whirlpool spun faster... emerald... turquoise… violet... black. Jade was being rushed along too, sucked down, Kyle's screams around her... And she knew she was heading toward the worst nightmare she could ever have imagined... Then she saw it, watched the treacherous water coiling, twisting, snaking inwards... she was being sucked toward a dark tunnel that vanished deep into the ocean…

…hurzjh... faadaw... oh...

14.
THE HOLLOW IN THE ROCKS

Kreh-ursh was awakened by the cold rising from the sand, which felt like rock beneath his sleeping mat. He sat up—body stiff, bones aching from a night spent under the stars. The sight of the fire, now just dead ashes, brought back the evening before. Taashou. Many of the images were muddled. He had questions to ask, but she was gone and had left no sign. In the early morning, with still one sixth part of a tide cycle remaining before sunrise, the beach was cold and gray. Abruptly then, that stumbling figure in the desert came to mind. He shut it out.

Behind him the island reared, sinister in the dawn. Its dark face, woven of shadowy vegetation, frowned down at the beach. Birds, just waking, began to screech. In moments the cacophony had reached its full power, but it sounded aggressive, alien. He didn't feel like beginning sea-nomad-becoming this morning, dreaded penetrating that matted jungle, had no desire to know what further secrets the island might be holding leashed, ready to pounce.

Yet hunger now attacked him; plus, he was thirsty. He had sand in his hair. It had sifted all through his clothes. He went down to the water and stripped, plunged under the waves. The shock of its chill refreshed him. To dry, he ran back and forth along the beach a few times. Then, squatting next to the dead fire, he nibbled some of the fish from the night before and took a swig of his mother's potion. Last night's meer-zjhur tasted bland; eating cold fish was not a great way to break your fast, but the potion refreshed. New energy flowed through his limbs. He rolled his sleeping mat, burying the dead fire under sand, and turned toward the jungle, searching for a way inland. Northward along the shore he wandered, the sand beneath his feet fine and pale, cool on his soles at this early time of the day.

As he walked, his mind returned to the visions. Given to all aspiring Shahee, they offered a glimpse of one's own personal possibilities, a kind of a guide, or maybe just an invention of one's own mind and hopes. His people were divided on where they came from. The shahiroh would not say. Did the sea callers prompt them? Could these visions really tell the future, or were they just imagined possibilities? Most people would not talk about what they had seen, considering them private and personal. Even his father was reticent:

"Kreh-ursh, it's a part of the event, of sea-nomad-becoming, and that is secret. Once you've experienced it, you can make up your own mind."

That did not help. Was that vision really how he

would die—far from the nearest drop of water, thirst slowly reducing him to dust? And what about the srehn-taagaag, or unicorns, the ritual on Kaa-meer-geh and the sea castle in the mountains? What did the scene with the sick child mean? Who, and where, was he? Strangest of all had to be ee-kawg-zjhur, the jewel fish. That is what he cannot understand. Ee-kawg-zjhur is not real. It was part of a children's story, a mythological being. None of it made sense.

The beach was small and soon gave way to a jumble of rocks leading out to a promontory. After scrambling over them a little way, he discovered a large, smooth hollow worn in the volcanic rock by ocean that no longer reached so high up the beach. The evening before, in his search for firewood, he had not come this far. It would have been a better place to camp. In the center, somebody—a candidate from an earlier year?—had built a round rock hearth. On one side, a narrow ledge had been carved from the stone and built up with rocks, a kind of sleeping alcove. The whole hollow was sheltered from sea breezes and would provide shade most of the day, except when the sun was at its highest. As surprising as the crude camp's existence might be, it was logical: Generations of his people had been coming here to complete the sea-nomad-becoming. His father might even have slept here, or any of his grandparents. He decided to camp here if he came back to the beach that night. It had a comforting feel, like an indirect link with home.

He was about to leave when a movement just beyond the hollow caught his eye. Too late, he realized... Something had thrashed about, then held itself still. He froze, not breathing. What was he thinking blundering about as if this were his own village? Here there were risks. Nothing, no sound came from beyond the hollow. Still, he slipped a knife from his bundle of tools. Edging around the rock wall, trying to find an angle from where he could see, he focused all his senses, but could only hear the rumble and hiss of surf on the reef... crackling jungle behind him. He crept closer. Maybe whatever was there had slithered or crept away. A few paces from the edge of the hollow, he leaned slowly forward, peering beyond the stone ridge that blocked his sight...

SCHLLICKEAAAARRGGHHH!

A dark shape flew up. A flaming brand tore past his head, singeing his ear. As he threw his weight back, his foot slipped. He struck with the knife, but the blade slid harmlessly. His hand touched hide and feathers as he fell. Head ringing, he rolled. Heat blasted him, scorching the rock where he had lain moments before. Springing up, knife arm out, he feinted sideways. He had to keep moving. Then he saw it… He froze.

It flew just a few paces and crashed into the far wall, blocking the exit. Glowing yellow eyes observed him. It shuffled, ungainly, blew out more flame. This time he dodged. Trapped together in the hollow among the rocks, Kreh-ursh and the dragon eyed each other warily.

15.
PATRICK

Jade!" She rested on hands and knees. On the step below the porch lay the shards of her muesli bowl: fruit, yogurt, and grains strewn across the driveway. Yet Kyle's screams kept ringing in her ears. She jumped up and ran into the house. As she entered her brother's room, his shrieks were cut off by another bout of vomiting. Jade grabbed the basin from the floor and whipped it under his face just as a torrent of deep green erupted from his throat. Joan was holding him, both hands tightly clasped around his body. Kyle kept retching before collapsing exhausted against his pillows. He immediately dropped whimpering into half-sleep.

"Thank you, Jade," Joan whispered. "You'd better leave us now."

She went out again, tipped the basin down the toilet and flushed it. Yuck. If only she hadn't let Kyle swim out! What was she thinking letting him stay in the water alone? Why hadn't she thought?

On the porch the sky glared at her, but she kept her head down, refusing to look. The clouds seemed to be expanding, a serrated swirling pattern that looked like nothing she'd ever seen. She felt as if she wanted to cry, to curl up in her bed and hide under the eiderdown, hoping this malignant… whatever it was… this evil force would disappear. Crouching down, she collected the remains of her breakfast off the steps, carried it inside, and dumped it in the trash. She would have to confess to the broken bowl, but now was not the time.

Undecided, she paused beside the stairs. From under the house came the dim whirrrrrr of Patrick's lathe and the schi-li-li-li-li-lick! of wood chips being sliced off a spinning post. The sound of that two-by-two gradually becoming a table leg was strangely reassuring, a background noise she had known since she was a kid. Its hum seduced. Patrick seemed to be treating this as a normal day. So she went downstairs and spent the morning watching him work.

Jade and Kyle's stepdad had lived with them since Kyle was two and Jade was six, though they still saw their real father a couple of weekends a month. Patrick was a wood-turner, spending all day in his workshop under the house, making furniture and ornamental stuff on his lathe. A steady, methodical man, his hands were knotted, rough, and scarred from years of work—chipping, chiseling, sanding, and caressing the wood into the shapes he wanted—looking like a pair of twisted roots themselves. Yet they had a surprising sensitivity, nimble and loving as they stroked or bashed along or against the grain. Patrick was tall, but his bench was low. When he was doing anything away from bench or lathe, he held a hooked stoop, like a heron perched, beak down, examining some life deep in the water below. His hair grew in tufts on each side of his head. His nose was also hooked like a beak, maybe more like a hawk's than a heron's, but his eyes were a pale honey color, so pale they were almost yellow, the clear hue of a kingfisher's gaze. There was something comforting about watching Patrick work. You got a feeling of safety. The world could be blown apart at any moment and you could be certain Patrick would still be there, peacefully carving and turning his beloved wood.

At ten-thirty, Jade went upstairs and prepared a snack for them all. During the holidays, if their mom was away, Jade made the morning snack and Kyle, the afternoon one. Patrick made lunch. Both Jade and Kyle were thankful for that, since—the truth had to be said: Patrick was a much better cook than their mom, who generally just beat some eggs together, threw them into a pan, burnt them to a crisp blackish brown, and scraped them onto plates. Jade and Kyle had learned the value of loads of tomato ketchup years ago. Today, Patrick and Jade had morning tea alone, while Joan continued to keep Kyle company. Jade was the first to see the muddy Range Rover turn into the driveway.

"Dr. Bilges is here!"

Patrick got up and showed him in, then disappeared down to his workshop. Jade wanted to follow the doctor into Kyle's room, but he shook his head and closed the door on her. She sat around, and when he and Joan finally came out, he was still giving his verdict:

"We probably didn't get all of that stuff when we pumped his stomach last night. That could be what is causing the irritation. Plus, he's caught a bit of an infection in his lungs—he was far too long in the water—hypothermia, from the cold out there. Deep water's surprisingly chilly, even in summertime. But he's a strong boy, and he's fighting it. I think you'll find he'll be as right as rain by tomorrow. But just to be sure, I'll come again this evening."

He paused.

"It's important at this point that you do keep a close eye on him. Give me a call on my cell if there's any change in his condition."

The doctor left. Joan went down to report to Patrick. Jade couldn't seem to occupy herself with any one thing. She started to read, but the words kept sliding away from her, and she had to reread each paragraph. Finally, she tossed her book aside and began playing a game on her cell phone; she got her lowest score yet. Downstairs, she could hear that Patrick was not doing any better. Every so often a black cloud of uncustomary swear words would drift up through the floorboards as her stepfather ruined yet another piece of good wood. He left off work early and came up to make lunch. The sandwiches the three of them sat down to were soggy and bland: overripe tomato slices sliding out of the crust, not enough salt, and mayonnaise that squirted onto the table when you bit into them.

"I really outdid myself this time, eh?"

But the other two were in no mood for jokes.

"What I should have done already is to report it to Wild Watch. I'll give Mr. Jackson a call after lunch," Joan decided.

Wild Watch was the local environmental group. Mr. Jackson, one of their neighbors, its president.

"But where could it have come from?" she continued, "We're not close to any shipping lanes."

"Don't forget the tides, or the prevailing wind. Every bit of flotsam on the ocean gets blown in here when the tide's right."

Joan looked doubtful: "There's something we're missing."

After lunch, Patrick went in and sat with Kyle while Joan went into her study and got on the phone. Jade left the house.

16. LESSER DRAGON

A lesser dragon, or eh-gawg-bhaanj. Its sharp beak was nonetheless the length of Krehursh's forearm, its feet armed with claws as long as his hand. It held itself still, wings draped limply across the rocks to either side. An odd scrap of flame puffed, defiant, from its gullet, but now Krehursh dodged its blasts easily, keeping a safe distance. He could see it was at the end of its strength. Unless he made some foolish movement, it would not attack. It was crippled: The normally cream and pink leathery quills of its wings, each longer than he was high, were plastered with dark sludge that weighed them down, making them useless for flight. Its body glistened in the same heavy mud. Only its head—vivid magenta crowned with a sapphire-blue crest—remained clean. But its long beak was caked with more of the filth.

He sheathed his knife. Although unsure how the majestic creature had got like that, the life code demanded he act. He edged carefully back toward the sleeping ledge, the reptile following his every move suspiciously. Yet it did not attack—nor retreat. It just looked exhausted.

Kreh-ursh dropped his belongings to the ground to lighten his load then, raising a cautious foot, stepped up onto the sleeping ledge. From there he reached toward the lip of the hollow, never taking his eyes from the dragon. The beast kept glaring. Once his hands had found their grip, he eased himself up the wall, out of the hollow. The lesser dragon, once it saw him retreat, lowered its head onto a muddy claw. It continued to track his movements with its baleful yellow eyes.

Free, the boy studied the tapestry of vegetation looming out over the shore. Above his camp, he saw a path leading up into the rainforest. For a moment, he felt odd, a feeling of being watched that made him hesitate. Unsheathing his knife once again, he clambered up the rocks, following that tenuous path into the jungle's gloom.

Under the trees another world flourished. Similar to his first vision of the night before, creepers hung wide from bough to branch, and thick-trunked ferns reached high above his head. Yet the light here was green-gray, an early morning haze of mist tendrils entwining trunks, a clear contrast to the gold-green sunlight-streaked forest of his vision. The trees were smaller: mainly palms, the only species capable of rooting into the thin topsoil and leaf mold covering the volcanic rock and coral so close to shore. The path twisted and turned up the back of a gradual rise, heading in the direction of the cone above, but Kreh-ursh stayed close to the shore, examining the nearby trees.

When he spied what he needed, he walked straight to the trunk... But flying in a dream was one thing; shimmying up that tree... He untied his belt from around his waist and retied it to form a loop, which he slipped halfway over both feet, positioning them on either side of the tree bole. Then he placed his hands around the trunk... and began to climb. His breath began to come in short gasps. He felt dizzy, his chest constricted. He worked his way slowly up: first his feet in their loop gripping the trunk on either side, then his hands reaching up and pulling his body higher, hugging the trunk so he could reposition his feet farther up. Looking up, he saw a bunch of bright purple berries close above. That meant he was now high... higher than he could imagine... Visions of his body thudding to earth threatened to paralyze him. Blood pounded through his veins as he tried to control his fear... If anyone else had been there... one of his mates... Kaar-oh loved climbing trees, but for Kreh-ursh it was always the same, this fear, the sweating, his blood pumping... Just get it over with. Carefully he reached out and plucked. The berries were growing on a plant that was itself wrapped around a vine. He put half a dozen in his pouch. Done. Now he could... What was that? He froze— something had definitely moved.

17.
THE LIFE CODE

Was there somebody down there? Kreh-ursh waited, listening, not daring to look down. It was silent. But he waited longer. Slowly the bush lost its hush. The birds resumed their racket. Whatever it was must have continued on its way. He began to ease his way down. It took forever. Then finally came that relief as his feet hit solid ground. His heart rate slowly returned to normal.

After retying his belt, he crept soft-footed on through the undergrowth. This time he kept his eyes lowered, studying the roots on the bush floor. Before long he found what he was looking for and gathered two large handfuls of a spongy red fungus growing around the base of a rotting stump. He moved stealthily on his way back to the shore. No sense alerting predators, or frightening the dragon. Yet that sense of being watched continued... He kept scanning the undergrowth. Nothing.

At the hollow he slid cautiously back down the wall. The bhaanj was still lying where he left it, one eye closed, the other lid raised barely enough to register his presence. From his bundle of belongings, he took a small wooden bowl and pounded the berries he had collected into a mush. He'd need at least five for this creature. He poured in a tiny amount of fresh water from the flask at his belt. When the mixture was evenly sloppy, he crumbled his remaining meer-zjhur in and kept blending it till it was a smooth paste. He scooped this fishy mixture out and tossed it carefully within the creature's reach, not wanting to risk getting back in range of its angry flames or threatening beak. He retreated to sit on the sleeping ledge and waited in stillness.

The dragon opened both eyes and studied the splatters of paste before it on the ground. For a long while it did nothing, not willing to trust the human-smelling mixture. Yet hunger got the better of it. Stretching out its head, it began to peck at the fish paste. Soon, the feathered reptile lay prone, struggling to keep its eyes open, aware it had been tricked off its guard, was now at the human's mercy. A last puff of flame and smoke erupted from its gullet. Its head crashed to the ground.

When he was sure the creature was really out cold, not just feigning to catch him off guard, Kreh-ursh approached. He poked it once with his toe, but it didn't budge. So he shouldered its bulk as best he could. Though as large as a taag—one of the sure-footed prairie beasts that the Taagaag-ee nomads rode in the south—it weighed no more than a child; this was a creature of the air, hollow bones supporting extended gaseous intestines, making it virtually weightless in flight. It smelled disgusting: its foul breath, the gases it burped and wheezed from its gullet, plus another unknown stink—heavy, acrid, like charcoal—the oozing mud that caked its body.

He hauled the dragon from the hollow and found a rock pool near the sea where he lay it down. It was truly awesome being so close to such a beast. Its feathered cape felt smooth, yet when he brushed his hand backward toward its crest, the quills bristled and its hide was rough like gravel. Easing its mouth open, he saw the rows of inwardly curving teeth and, right at the back, close to its jowl pouch—where it collected the gas it produced—two jagged, flint-like canines it gnashed together for sparks to ignite its blasts.

He dipped the fungus he had collected in seawater and rubbed it between his hands until it formed a soapy lather. He applied this to the creature's feathers, and the suds helped to wash off the mud. Yet cleaning the beast was difficult. He was not sure how long the sedative would last. The scum was tough to remove, sticking like glue to both the quills and his own hands.

Having lost track of how long he worked, he was aware only of every muscle beginning to ache, of his arms feeling like they wanted to fall from his body. All the time, that sense of being watched... he could not shake it... Yet the bush canopy revealed nothing. Reaching out, his mind encountered nobody nearby. Could it be Taashou? If anybody was there, they were hiding themselves well.

Suddenly, the sleeping beast snorted, showering

him in a disgusting cloud of ash. His time was up. He looked at his handiwork. Most of the slime was gone from the beast's wing feathers and beak, but a faint dark ring still clung to its body. He did not dare sit beside it any longer. As if to confirm his fears, the dragon reared its head, staring directly at him. Kreh-ursh mind-punched, hurling himself back even as flame surged from between the creature's jaws. As he flew through the air, he was aware of another mind alongside his own, also punching at the dragon's brain, forcing its flaming maw aside. Kreh-ursh scrambled back just in time. He was barely a few paces distant when the dazed creature turned its head again, focusing its fiery eyes, and spat another blast of flame. As Kreh-ursh and the other being mind-punched together again, to deter its aim, the boy rolled farther back. The flame seared a patch of lichen on the rocks he had just left, crisping it instantly. He dashed into the hollow, grabbed his belongings, and raced up into the trees.

Hidden under ferns, he watched as the reptile slowly continued to wake. That other presence hovered, familiar. The dragon looked his way as it began to struggle to its feet, but woozy from the sedative, it overbalanced and fell. Only on the third attempt could it stand shakily. After staring toward the forest for a moment, head on one side, it began to clean the remaining fungus-soap from its feathers. Standing, it was a magnificent creature, as tall as Kreh-ursh himself. When it spread its wings, they arched up to almost twice its height. Kreh-ursh withdrew farther into the tree cover… That was when he saw her. He scrambled through ferns, ripping creepers from his path:

"Geh-meer!"

But she was gone. He called with his mind. No answer. She had broken the rite. Candidates must not help each other. Each was alone to succeed or fail. Yet without her, he might now be dragon food. Turning, he got a last glimpse through the trees of the majestic beast perched on the ridge of the hollow, stretching and flapping its wide wings mightily. Then with a great leap, it threw itself into the air and began to rise, circling. He watched it negotiate the breeze, find an updraft, and soar up, away behind the island, a pink, sun-bright sail planing sideways across the blue morning sky. He sighed. The sight of such a wondrous reptile… that was what gave meaning to the life code.

18.
SHADOWS WITHIN

The boy headed inland along the track he had found earlier, the vegetation gradually changing as he climbed higher along the ridge. Although the slope was not steep, he was soon panting from the effort. His thoughts continued to dwell on the eh-gawg-bhaanj. Lesser dragons often fished the lagoons and wider ocean, but they always returned to their nesting ground among the volcanoes. Kreh-ursh had never seen one up close. What was that stuff on its wings? He had seen nothing like it, no mud that stuck like that, heavy enough to keep a powerful creature like the dragon out of the skies. It must have come from somewhere on Zjhuud-geh, which was the only land close by.

Soon, he saw through a gap in the trees that he had climbed high above the lagoon. The water below was a clear turquoise, stretching to the white halo of the surrounding reef. Schools of fish flitted to and fro above the sandy bottom like cloud shadows. Occasionally, a larger fish, cruising hawk-like, circled around, a gray presence gliding, somber, through the shallows. Ocean breakers crashed violently against the reef, and far out the sea was deep blue flecked with puffs of white where wind clipped the tops off the highest waves. Shoals of kree-eh created mauve and green ribbons through the deep water. The sun was now high in the sky and filtered down through the trees to where he rested, providing a gentle warmth that set the vegetation steaming.

Abruptly, he sat up, eyes narrowed against the glare off the sun-bright sea, straining to see out. In the distance, almost at the horizon, was an indefinite smudge. Too dark, too large, for a school of fish, too hazy for a canoe—he was puzzled. Almost imperceptibly, as he watched, the shadow on the water drifted farther off until he could no longer make it out.

He turned his thoughts back to sea-nomad-becoming. This was what he must crack, what he was here for. He decided to consult his vision. Squatting on the track, he began to undo the bag hanging from his neck, but the drawstring momentarily snarled with Kaar-oh's. He took the scarlet bag from around his neck and held Kaar-oh's carved talisman in his palm for a moment.

Then he was back there, living through the accident again—Kaar-oh falling toward the green water, that same crimson bag swinging against his brown skin... white tunic... stained red... and scarlet clouds mushrooming out through the shallows.

"Kaar-oh!"

His friend was reaching out... that look of shock and fear in his eyes as he realized he could not regain the safety of the canoe...

Kreh-ursh blocked the vision, aware once more of his friend's absence. He slid the boy's talisman back under his tunic as he felt that ache knotting his guts again. Why were things like this! Why wasn't Kaar-oh here now, attempting sea-nomad-becoming? Yet his friend had gone for good. These memories… were just memories… but they were all that now remained.

Wiping his sight clear, he slid his own carving out into his hands. The delicate wooden shape brought his concentration back, and he cleared his mind of everything except that first image he'd seen with Taashou—he slipped into trance. Little by little, the figure in his hands began to feel warm. Soon it was firmly drawing him, a hot weight in his palms pulling, pulling, as if it wanted to escape from his hands, dropping to the left. He turned that way... Yes, it was pulling him to the left. He half-opened his eyes, searching for a path leading in that direction. There was nothing off the track but a wall of lush ferns and, lower down in a slight valley, a stand of taller trees that poked above the surrounding growth. They attracted him, for no reason other than a vague intuition. Returning his amulet to its pouch, he pushed off the track and moved down the slope toward them.

At first it was difficult to make progress. Ferns and undergrowth formed a barrier that stopped him advancing, but gradually he entered a different type of jungle. Here the trees reached higher and wider than they did on the ridge, with more space between the trunks. There were fewer plants growing on the bush floor. These were bhaa-shot trees—their fat, spherical boles curving up into three or four thick boughs that held clusters of limp, purplish fronds. The large, yellowish fruit they produced, once cooked, was succulent and nourishing. Kreh-ursh forced himself to conquer his fear again—though the bhaa-shot weren't quite as tall as the trees he had climbed on the coast— and shimmy up, carefully avoiding the bark's knifelike spines. He knocked down three fruit. Back on the ground he stowed them in a net bag he had tucked in his belt. He continued on his way. The much sparser undergrowth at ground level made progress easier, but the fallen, rotting fronds could be slippery underfoot.

He walked through the jungle, keeping the upslope leading to the volcano on his right. The terrain and plant life continued to change subtly, the bhaa-shot grove giving way to stands of bheem-aa, straight, rough-barked trees with small needle-shaped leaves, and lohn-goh, a strong-wooded variety with flaky bark scales and small rhomboid-shaped leaves. Clusters of pale yellow and red rree-taa flowers hung from tree forks or curled around the snaking vines, providing bright spots of color against the green and brown forest. Bird life was prolific. Wide-tailed lehk and acrobatic, blue-breasted keh-moh flitted through the bush space hunting for insects. Once he disturbed a large mehrr-koh, which blundered screeching from tree to tree before flapping heavily away, the scarlet and purple of its back and wing feathers contrasting sharply with the rich yellow hues on its breast.

After walking for a long time, up ahead to his right, Kreh-ursh spied one: a taat-eh tree, a single one. His tree, the kind he was looking for! He climbed toward it. It was a mature specimen, possibly over a hundred years old. The solid, fast-growing trunk, wider than he was high, soared straight out of the ground into the highest treetops. He placed a hand on the smooth, waxy bark and knew he was getting close. He pushed on ahead. Soon he saw others, and before long, the taat-eh were the only kind of tree surrounding him. He stopped for a while and, closing his eyes, summoned again the visionary picture of his own tree strongly into his mind.

Opening his eyes, he knew it was there. He couldn't actually see it yet, but he sensed it was close by. He took two steps forward, looked around, and this time he did see it. Partly hidden by two thick trunks on his left, it was growing a short distance farther down the slope, close to the edge of a small clearing. He laughed. It seemed so easy just to have stumbled on it like this, exactly as he saw it in his vision. Even though he had spent weeks in training classes in his village preparing for this part of the test, he had doubted it would ever work exactly as it was meant to. He half ran, half bounded down the slope and slapped his hands against the trunk, the trunk of his tree! He imagined he could feel an answering vibration through the wood, a kind of affirmation, saying, "That's right, I'm yours. Let's get to work!" He stood beside his trunk feeling awed, almost frightened. The first part of his ritual—of Shahee-faadaw, the sea-nomad-becoming—was a success.

19.
TWILIGHT CROSSER

Lilac and tangerine clouds hung above the indigo sea. Taashou stood on a low promontory of rocks that extended westward into the lagoon, scanning the flashing breakers striking the reef, just visible in the fading light. She waited, noting the first, bright evening stars shining in the twilit canopy. Swarms of hazy constellations had begun to light the dark when her attention was grabbed by a massive shape moving beyond the surf.

I await you.

To show her position, she opened a tiny clay fire pot she had held concealed under her cloak. Before long, she discerned a figure swimming in through the lagoon. She turned and walked back along the rocks onto the beach, holding the lantern up to guide the swimmer in. Then she stood before the whispering tide, amid wrack and driftwood. The swimmer waded from the waves.

Daakohn, at last we can talk!

Taashou, it is good to see you again.

I have a fire above.

They walked up the sand arm in arm. While Taashou was wrapped tightly in her blue shahiroh's cloak against the evening chill, Daakohn was dressed as before, in his close-fitting suit of what looked like kelp but hugged his body like supple leather. He did not seem to notice the cold, though when they came to the low fire laid in a sheltered lee of the beach, he squatted close and warmed himself as if he had spent an age exposed to the harshest elements.

One can adjust and adapt to life in the depths, but nothing replaces a healthy blaze!

I was thinking of you when I built it up.

When alone, they always spoke in mind speech, swifter for communicating both thoughts and feelings though tricky to shield from prying attention.

How are the candidates faring?

They have just begun. Two are highly promising yet both troublesome in their way. I cannot work it out. I have decided to monitor them closely.

No hurzjh-faadaw-oh among them?

Do we need a hurzjh-faadaw-oh?

The imbalance in the rift will not heal itself. Since we last spoke, it has become worse. Now all the Shahee feel it. It affects the kree-eh the most. And when the kree-eh die, so does the ocean. Something must be done.

Yet how can we know what? I will go myself. I have a better chance...

You cannot, Taashou. You are old and have been too long a part of this world. You would not be able to cross.

Then we will close it... if we can. I refuse to send an

innocent into the twilight crossing, to exile them from everything they have known, their sense of belonging— forever—and even if they return, to spend what remains of their days like some cast-off piece, disconnected from tribe and culture...

Like me? Knowledge has its own price, Taashou. I chose my destiny.

You were seventeen. Yours was by accident, not design —you have said so yourself.

Daakohn drew a burning stick from the fire and began to play with it in the night air, drawing patterns as if it were a wand.

Still, we all choose, perhaps not our pasts but certainly our futures. The memories I love best from my former life... riding my mount like the wind across the plains, traveling with my people, the Taagaag-ee, to our summer camp, the celebrations... I will never have them back.

You could, Daakohn! Talk to Raa-gehd; go back to your people...

You know I cannot. My mount, my companion, is another now, and he is not suited to the grassy plains. So I wander, a nomad among nomads. We are all alone— the way we are born, the way we die—but for the twilight crosser, doubly so, because I lack that part of me that stayed in his world.

He threw the stick into the fire:

It is always thus, but I would not have had it any other way. In a sense I still chose my life. Yet you, Taashou, do not have any choice in this. An older person cannot go. It must be somebody young enough to shed the trappings of this world with no remorse, one who has not grown roots deep enough to bind.

Taashou frowned. *Like the tree in the myth, uprooted from the valley and sent to grow forever alone on the mountain to stop the sky from falling in?*

You can mock, Daakohn smiled, *but that is how it is. You cannot rip somebody from their universe, throw them into another to breathe alien air or gas or whatever and then transplant them back again without some damage occurring.*

They were both silent, studying the fire as if waiting for it to speak and offer answers. Then Taashou turned and looked at the older man. *Why?*

Why? In what sense, why?

You became hurzjh-faadaw-oh by accident. The rift healed itself that time. How do we know the same will not happen? What is different this time?

Some force is pulling the kree-eh from our seas. It is not the same, not the same at all.

So, the hurzjh-faadaw-oh.

The twilight crosser must be absolutely without hesitation. Remembering, Daakohn shuddered. *The very knowledge of this thing induces a fear so strong that most grown Shahee could not overcome their instinct for survival to chance it.* He looked at Taashou. *You will have to find someone young... young yet ... ruthless, brave... talented yet foolhardy.*

I will search out a volunteer. But I will not sacrifice an innocent, Daakohn. That would be an abomination. It must be somebody who fully knows where they are going and the slim chance of any return.

I went without knowing. That was what, in a strange way, saved me.

As you say, this time it is different.

They sat in silence after that. The fire gradually died.

20.
A KEEN-SKUR'S FANG

Looking up at the trunk, Kreh-ursh should have been happy; he had his tree. His success at locating it had renewed his faith in himself, in his training. There ought to be no doubts now. Yet there was something… Geh-meer being there down at the coast… that sick dragon… and something, or someone else… This island… it made him nervous; it felt creepy.

The trunk, slightly wider than his shoulders, as in his vision, stretched up above him, perfectly straight, for two or three lengths of his own body. It was perfect. Its crown spread into a dense tangle of smaller branches and tiny spade-shaped leaves. He only had to place his hand on the bark to feel immediate empathy with the thing growing beside him, the joy of its living sap flowing beneath his fingertips. Yet thinking about the practical problems to overcome, he felt unsure. They were high above the water. It was impossible to move the tree down to the shore. So he would have to work up here.

He took a swallow of his potion and looked around. Since he had left home, he had drunk a lot of the liquid. He must start hunting and gathering food. To one side of the small clearing an old root system thrust up new shoots from a hewn stump. It looked as if some other candidate had performed sea-nomad-becoming here. A brook slapped and rattled its pebbled bed beyond. When he went to investigate, he found the stream ran swift, free of debris, a clean roadway back to the sea. It was perfect, yet… something about this clearing stirred memories. Crazy—it was the first time he had ever walked these slopes.

Placing gourd, sleeping mat, and his bag of tools to one side of the clearing, he went back into the jungle with just his knife. A cautious search around his campsite showed that the area was safe enough: no recent signs of any large beasts. He set bird snares and gathered a small supply of roots, berries, and fruit, hanging them away from predators on low tree boughs back at his new camp.

The next job was building a rudimentary bivouac from sticks and vines. After harvesting several armfuls of kaank leaves—long, flat, and fibrous—he sat in the clearing and wove until sunset. This large triangular matting would not only roof his bivouac while he stayed here—once it had dried fully, it would also have another use. The bivouac, shaded by trees on one side of the clearing, was hardly permanent, but should hold up well enough as a shelter and somewhere to store his gear. Enough for the days he would be here. After a simple meal of berries and fruit, he crawled into his bivouac and collapsed as darkness fell.

Early next morning he approached the trunk of his tree. Laying out his tools beside him, he placed his hands on the bark, preparing to work. His feeling of oneness with the wood was renewed. A thrum of life hummed in the flowing sap. This was the blood he tried to connect with, asking this life force for permission to meet his needs, as he initiated the next, longest, most strenuous stage of Shahee-faadaw.

Evening sun rays slanted down through the leaves, gilding the clearing gold and bronze. Kreh-ursh lay exhausted on the ground. He knew he should crawl under shelter to protect himself from the dampness night would bring, but he could not lift even a finger. Beside him, stretching the length of the clearing, lay his tree. The mass of its branches was tangled in the dense undergrowth on the far side of the clearing. On this side, the lower end of its trunk, hacked into a rough cone by many blows from his ax, lay close to its stump. Wood chips carpeted the surrounding ground for some distance. His muscles ached, and his hands were blistered. Tonight he could do no more.

Sleep claimed him quickly but brought little relief. His troubled dreams carried him back to Rrurd, to the past. In this memory-lit space, Kaar-oh was there. The boy sat simply, cross-legged on the ground in his ill-fitting, berry-stained tunic. His lop-sided grin showed the blank gap of his missing tooth as he improvised another of those crazy ideas they both knew would lead to trouble. Kreh-ursh had been punished once already this moon by the Shahee Council—Rrurd's gaggle of puffed-up elders, whose only activity seemed to be spying on Kreh-ursh and Kaar-oh, trying to stop them from having any fun.

In his dreams they were back in the canoe at the river mouth, under a midday sun that struck like a spear from above. Arm length by careful arm length, they reeled out the thin fibrous rope. Bound at intervals along it were bloody hunks of meat, each chunk concealing a gaark-teer or hook-star—the five-pronged, barbed piece of ironwork designed to wedge in the beast's gullet. Then they squatted in the bottom of the canoe, scanning the green surface. The river was dead still.

"Maybe we should have asked permission," Kaar-oh murmured.

"You know what they would have said: The river Gaa-shuudot is out of bounds till we're full Shahee."

"What are we supposed to do then? We need it to become men…"

"You can complete sea-nomad-becoming without it."

"But it helps. Anyway, it was your idea. Don't you want it now?

"Of course, I want it… I just wonder… maybe we should just practice working with the wind or the currents—you know, forget about the… it."

"But you're the one who wanted to try—can't you imagine the way the chants will work, focused through a keen-skur fang? We'll be more than Shahee, we could end up as, as…"

Words failed him. Then, again he saw Kaar-oh falling, saw that crimson pouch against his pale rough-spun tunic, a look of fear, a spout of blood—a scarlet splash pumping into the river water, gathering predators…

He was awake. It was deep night. On the sacred island. Trees were groaning, boughs creaking. Forms and shadows, like clouds, like people, flitted and drifted between the trunks around him. Wisps of mist glowed silvery. Kreh-ursh could see him approaching through the trees… A face came near, smiling, whispering. Silky fingers seemed to drag through his hair…

This time he was truly awake. This was real. Taashou was leaning over him. She had a gourd of liquid she placed to his lips. It tasted similar to his mother's potion, though there were other strange flavors. Opening her hand, she revealed a half-dozen gohrroh-urbh leaves.

Chew. Don't swallow. Then spit them out.

He ground the herb between his teeth, extracting as much juice as possible before spitting the pulp outside the bivouac. The leaves were rich and flavorful. Yet even as he reached for another, their heaviness hit him. His eyelids drooped, his hand dropped to the mat, head falling onto his improvised pillow, and he slipped back into sleep. This time, there were no dreams. He slept soundly, deeply, deliciously. The next morning he was woken by the cacophony of birds, who screamed their laughter at him. They found it hilarious, the crazy things a body could imagine in the night.

21.
SEATOWN

When she was sure the boy was sleeping soundly, Taashou crept out of the bivouac and moved with soft steps down through the dark jungle toward the shore. Troubling whispers and sighs stirred the trees around her on all sides. Occasionally, she saw wraithlike beings drifting in the jungle. She took care to avert her eyes. Yet once, a ghostly figure—an ancient man, wisps of pale silver hair dripping from his crinkled head, a heavy staff clasped firmly in both hands—appeared from behind a tree and confronted her. She spoke before he did:

Father, I have a task to perform. Let me on my way. We will have our reckoning when I return.

Taashou... Even in mind speech, his voice wheezed like spray on the rocks. *I'm not here for one of our little battles; I must warn you—the rift...*

I know. I've summoned the Great Council. The rift has returned. Shah is threatened.

Not just Shah. The rift is random—it appears where it will. Worlds meet and flow apart—the timeless fertilization of the universe between dimensions... but an imbalance has occurred. You must look deeper. This is not just a threat to the sea.

The land people have been called as well.

Yes, the Rraawu and other peoples should have a voice. They may be next.

The only reason Gordonor is coming is to seal a trading agreement with the Geyg-ee...

Then that is a gift the universe has given you; make use of it. The Shahee cannot solve this alone.

So what path?

You know I cannot advise action from this side.

But you can see further. You have escaped time. Tell me more.

A silence fell while they studied each other. Finally, the old man spoke:

The rift is natural. It comes and goes with the years. Yet something on the other side... This is not natural.

But who could wield such power?

I can say no more. When we lose our place in your dimension, we are shunned by the laws that rule it and can no longer influence events. Yet your world is endangered. You must act.

Taashou was silent for a long time, gazing into the night as she thought. Then:

The boy you see sleeping there, watch him while I'm away. He must finish Shahee-faadaw.

The old man laughed:

The lad's complicated things for himself, fighting his future and his past together! Go, Taashou. One of the others is also more important than you think... One of the girls...

Geh-meer?

He nodded. *She has the Sight, like yourself. All three—there was a third, but he is with me now—are important. But go, finish your task... They'll be safe under my watch... Though remember to return... or I shall bring you back.*

As he spoke, his figure faded into the night.

At the shore, the shahiroh pulled away the dry palm leaves covering her canoe. Suu-ohn-maalaa—Sighing Seabird—the craft she had lovingly built all those years ago, on this very isle. The vessel seemed to sing a welcome as she slid it across the hissing silver sand. It slipped into the lapping waves.

Ahead of them, the water was a black vacuum in the night. Only the long, low cloud of surf glowing out on the reef guided her. Driving her paddle into the sea, she headed toward it. Spray erupted and rained down, drenching her as she entered the collision zone between ocean breakers and the coral shelf. Then her chant prevailed, water boiled under her craft, raising her, easing her across the violence. Soon she was slicing out through the night. Above her Hurm's Girdle shone rosy, while the White Lady was a slim crescent low in the sky. Kree-eh glowed silver and pink through the black water. Reading the stars, Taashou turned Suu-ohn-maalaa north. Her chant rose in volume, becoming strident, thunderous above the roar and moan of Shah. She struggled up the shivering black slopes, sliding fast down into their valleys. Always to the same purpose, reaching for the same destination.

A sixth of a tide cycle later, a spark flashed on the horizon. She lost it as she plunged over another crest and dropped down. Yet soon it was back, flickering in the distance. Before long, though still a long way off, she saw it clearly: a constant flame burning in the night.

I'll be waiting for you on the dock. Before Duu-feen left her cabin, she raked the fire down and secured the guard. She threw the sea-green cloak of the Shahee around her shoulders and wrapped it tight. Here on the high ocean, the wind gusted chill at night, even in summer. After fastening her door, she made her way across Shah-rraatawuu toward the docks. Around her, despite the time, the place seethed with activity. Shahee strode to and fro, escorting the guests who had been arriving all day. Close-lipped shahiroh stepped quietly around the shaky land people who'd invaded their domain: portly Rraawuu from the cities and lithe but tremulous Geyg-ee, whose bows and spears seemed oddly out of place on the ocean. Most looked green, nauseated, struggling to find their balance in this, their first experience at sea.

The floating town was built on rafts in the form of a huge wheel. Carved hulls with platforms lashed between them formed its body. Each hull could be steered individually to best meet the forces of wind and tide while remaining attached to the whole flexible structure. When the community needed to travel, this seaborne town did not turn, but each hull was steered, keels dropped and sails raised. The town would lumber along its course, aided by shahiroh skill. Fore and aft—though those terms were ambiguous here—higher, arched structures created two gaps in the ring, raised so that even a large canoe might pass beneath with masts lowered. Inside the wheel, the "docks"—wooden platforms floating on the sea, bound to the inside of the ring—allowed vessels to be tied up, lashed fast during storms. The town moved fluidly—while one rim crested a high ocean roller, the other might be washing the shallows of a trough. This aspect was what most scared the land people, that at any moment those boards might separate on the waves and sink beneath their feet. Duu-feen knew that was ridiculous. Everything was built of the lightest wood, bound with lee-aandeh cord. The town was like a floating garland of woven twigs, sprightly buoyant and capable of adapting to the ocean's every mood.

Tonight, the main mast was raised and the beacon lit —a single enormous taat-eh spar that towered over the ocean, visible from far out to sea. It was mounted on the widest platform in the ring—a huge raft a hundred paces wide. Dozens of fine lee-aandeh weed stays held it upright. What the land people did not see was that a spar of almost half its length, weighted with rock ballast, dropped down into the depths beneath to steady the whole structure.

Duu-feen's cabin was located on the opposite side from the dock where she knew the other woman would arrive. As she moved through town, she greeted Shahee, shahiroh, and other sea peoples. A gang of kids swarmed past her, having taken advantage of the confusion the visitors had brought to escape beds and guardians. Apart from Shah-rraatawuu's habitual residents, Shahee had come from Rrurd, from Rraam-taw, and most of the other villages up and down Shah's coast and far-flung islands.

When she reached the dock, she dropped her cloak in a dry nook and swung herself down onto the wave-washed platform using a guideline. At that moment, a huge roller was passing through the town and the dock lagoon had swelled into a rounded, glassy hill. A sleek canoe glided over its crest. She had come in unseen under the forward bridge port. Duu-feen's heart thumped. She smiled at her own reaction.

Hoh-ee, stranger.

The figure in the stern of the craft smiled back.

Hoh-ee, Duu-feen.

I have missed you, Taashou.

22.
COMING TO COUNCIL

After so many years, Duu-feen still felt an intense fluttering in her ribcage each time they were about to meet. Suu-ohn-maalaa cruised in as the town traversed the wave trough, flooding the docks thigh deep in swell. Duu-feen fought to keep her feet and grabbed the canoe as it surged toward her. Then the shahiroh had jumped out and together they ran the vessel up the ramp, lashing it fast under the lee of the ring platform as the town rose and water streamed away. Drenched to the skin, they gave each other a tight hug. Taashou was shivering.

"Acchh, girl, you'll kill yourself if you don't take more care to keep dry out there. Why do you think cloaks were invented?"

"I like to feel the surf on my skin."

"You aren't immortal, you know."

"So many years now, I've been doing this, supervising sea-nomad-becoming. Yet lately I seem to get more creaks and pains in my bones every day."

"No surprise if you won't keep wrapped up better. Come back to the cabin and warm up. I've got supper prepared."

"No, I have to check on the council—make sure

everybody's turned up.

"That's taken care of. Lehd has it under control. You've got half a tide cycle before you need to be anywhere. Come back to the cabin."

Taashou submitted silently. Duu-feen helped her up from the dock.

ecause no cabin in town was large enough for the Great Council, the central market had been cleared from the main platform. A brisk sea breeze ruffled the people gathered, each community's representatives, who were seated on benches under the open sky. While dawn crept pink over one edge of the raft, night grayly retreated off the other. The chill stopped anyone from nodding off so early in the morning.

They were strange, the land people gathered here, so conscious of the threatening ocean around them. Some, Duu-feen saw, did not look half so sickly as they had the night before, but Gordonor, fat delegate-elect of the Rraawuu city of Solgom, had to be hauled onto the platform on a litter. His normally purple face showed a greenish hue, and his red and gold tunic was flecked with vomit. His skinny assistant was no better. Duu-feen suppressed a giggle as the two men leaned over the same bucket at the same time. Heads cracked. Gordonor swore at his helper, regaining his normal color for a moment. Then the town crested another wave and began to lurch downward again. Both men groaned. It had been unwise to call the meeting at Shah-rraatawuu. It was obvious the land people would be laid low with seasickness their first few days on the ocean.

Duu-feen saw Taashou come onto the raft. The shahiroh looked around, then went to a seat well upwind of Gordonor and his vomit-speckled group. She looked fiercer than ever. Duu-feen knew her expression was a mask for the real worry she felt at what she had to achieve here.

"I'm sure you must be laughing, Taashou!" Gordonor looked furious, sitting up on his stretcher, eyes almost popping from his head. "You think it's a great joke, don't you? Dragging us all out here onto this raft in the middle of a storm. That isn't how you'll get my cooperation for your schemes."

She was unruffled: "Not mine, Gordonor—ours. This affects you as much as anyone. But are you serious about a storm? You know, I think you're right—there could be one on its way."

Taashou frowned at the horizon. Gordonor wailed and collapsed back into his pillows. Now the light was bright. Most of the other representatives had arrived, accepting the benches reserved for them. Raa-geh-ur was there, tiny and sprite, leader of the Taagaag-ee, the horse nomads of the southern plains. He and his people seemed less affected by the rolling ocean. Maybe wave movement was not so different from the loping gait of their creatures.

Raa-geh-ur was greeting Eloh-inderash, the lean, brown shepherd of the Geyg-ee, from the lower slopes of Geh-urbh-Geh-ot, when there was a rushing of air that rose above the ocean's roar and crash, outdoing the wind's whistling. People looked around, bewildered, saw nothing. The shepherds were the first to look up, cry out, and dart for cover, unslinging bows, notching arrows on the run.

"Hold! Relax! These are friends, here for the same reasons we are!" Taashou's voice carried over the gathering. People froze. She seemed to have grown to twice her normal height. Her presence commanded.

Then down into the open space in the platform's center swept three huge, pink and golden bhaanj, skillfully avoiding the mast stays. The wide leathery membranes that served them for wings seemed to stretch the entire width of the raft, while their bloated bodies rippled and floated gently down onto the deck. Flickering golden eyes scanned the crowd, and a yellow scrap of flame curled from the odd snout.

"Sheen-gaw aleef!" cried a voice. The dragons settled down, calmer despite being hemmed in by so many humans. From between the wings of each beast a rider emerged: booted, dressed in leather, and muffled against the chill of the upper atmosphere. Their leader sprang from her mount's broad back, surveyed the gathering, then spying the shahiroh, she stepped forward:

Taashou!

The old woman smiled. "Kehl-grehnaa. Welcome."

As they hugged, Duu-feen felt a surge of heat rise through her. She barely had time for surprise that the dragon rider had used mind speech. Who was this woman who was so intimate with Taashou? She was stout, maybe ten years older than Duu-feen's thirty years. It was almost with relief that she saw another of the dragon riders move up beside Kehl-grehnaa and place a hand on her shoulder in a familiar way. The man was tall and broad, red-brown hair cut to shoulder length. Duu-feen was too far away to hear their conversation, but Kehl-grehnaa seemed to be introducing the man to Taashou.

Then suddenly Gordonor's storm arrived. A maelstrom erupted in the center of the dock lagoon. Water boiled. Waves lifted and washed across the docks, even up onto the pontoons, swamping the deck platforms. Wood and cables screeched and wailed as they were wrenched about in the ocean's turmoil. The three dragons lifted up in fright and swept away, circling far out around the town. Everyone turned toward the center of the lagoon. The entire floating town of Shah-rraatawuu was heaved and shaken. Only the steadiest Shahee kept their feet. That was why they were the first to see it: a rearing, twisting, snakelike body, wide as a bhaanj's wingspan, its terrible horns, eight or ten of them, sprouting from its ugly face; a necklace of tentacles writhed about the scaly body as it heaved itself from the water, up, up, high into the air, reaching toward the mainmast and higher, higher, finally twice its height. It roared, blowing its fetid, salty breath across the town.

"Hoh-ee!" shouted Taashou, her voice a mere whisper above the serpent-beast's pant: "How you love to make an entrance!"

23. WAVECRAFT, WINDCALLER

As soon as Kreh-ursh awoke—mist surrounding him, a silver screen on which gray trunks were projected like stone columns in an ancient temple—he sipped a few drops of his mother's potion and swallowed some berries to renew his energy. When he checked his snares, he found he had caught two mehrr-koh. He released the younger. The life code allowed him to take just as much as he needed for his own sustenance. While he worked, resetting traps, then killing and plucking the plump bird, the sun shot slender rays through the vapor until it was torn to ragged shreds that fluttered away on the insistent breeze. He worked without pause, trying to keep his mind busy. Yet his thoughts returned to dwell on last night's dreams, on Kaar-oh. His friend's presence haunted him here like never before. Zjhuud-geh, this island, played tricks, magnified emotions, twisted them until you could not work out what was real and what was not. He had thought he was getting over the death. Geh-meer had convinced him this would be good for him, to continue with sea-nomad-becoming. It would help him overcome that guilt, that captivity to Kaar-oh's memory. Now it felt as if he would never be free.

The sun was high by the time he got to work on his trunk. First he stripped off branches and bark until he was left with a bare, wooden column. Some time after midday, using ax, mallet, and wedges, he began to split this into plank-like sections. Taat-eh wood, though springy and flexible, split easily. By sunset, he had five rough planks of more or less equal thickness and varying width. Still he forced himself on, working beyond the limit he felt himself capable of until the fading light forced him to build a small fire and spit some of the mehrr-koh.

In his dreams that night, he wandered again through fitful, scrappy memories. Yet early on, it began to rain, awakening him. His bivouac was not perfect at keeping out the wet. In his fight to stay dry, he ended up huddling cross-legged, blanket wrapped close, listening to the risa-risa-ris of rain attacking the jungle canopy, the toc-tic-cli-clic of heavy droplets falling from vine to leaf to forest floor. In that close, clamorous night, Kaar-oh crowded back into his mind.

Here he was, here they both were, he and Kaar-oh, arguing with Geh-meer because she would not get involved with their expedition. They were sitting outside Geh-meer's hut, dry under the roof overhang while rain dripped off the eaves above them and drove in gray sheets across the bay. The overturned canoes down on the beach, pulled up onto the shingle and nesting among kelp and driftwood, looked like sleek, brown kee-leh—the amphibious creatures that lived in colonies on the rocky promontories to the south.

"You are not going down to Gaa-shuudot—tell me you aren't. You boys would be dumber than dumb to think about doing that."

"It's only a river. We're more or less Shahee now. We'll be able to anyway in a few moons' time."

"Kreh-ursh, Kaar-oh, you're not allowed! Next you'll be telling me you're off to hunt the keen-skur."

"Are there keen-skur down there?"

The look Kaar-oh gave him told Kreh-ursh that his pretended innocence had fallen flat. You couldn't really fool Geh-meer.

"It's a stupid idea, way too dangerous. Even the Shahee leave the keen-skur alone."

Kreh-ursh was secretly relieved. Maybe they could forget it now. It gave him a way out. Yet he found himself arguing, defending himself.

"I could get a fang—I know how. I've got a plan."

And Kaar-oh backed him up. "I'm in. Not for the fang —it's just the extra sailing. We need the practice."

With Kaar-oh set to go, that was half the battle won.

"It won't help you with sea-nomad-becoming. It's stupid. You're just looking for trouble. And it's against the life code: if you don't need it, you can't hunt it."

"Need is relative. Maybe we do. It's the challenge."

"You don't need a keen-skur's fang. No one uses one. People still come back Shahee. A hunt to capture a keen-skur—you might not come back from that."

Then a strange thing happened: Geh-meer stopped, staring fixedly at a point—her eyes blank. Suddenly, she returned, but now there was fear and urgency in her voice: "Kaar-oh! Don't go! You mustn't! Kreh-ursh, back me up. Tell him! Tell him not to go!"

Kaar-oh lashed out: "What? Do you think I'm scared? We're going!"

How could she have known? When they set off, in the grayness of early dawn, that vivid expectation of adventure they thought they would feel was missing, replaced by a tight fear that they were sneaking away like cowards. They knew that Geh-meer would not say anything to the adults, but the sense of bravado with which they had thought up the plan had somehow faded away like morning mist.

However, once free of Rrurd lagoon, the sea breeze raised their spirits. It blew away doubt. The excitement of the journey infected them. Both boys were skilled sailors. Though the village canoe they'd borrowed—one of a few communal craft used for training—was not the fastest, they had enough skill, along with vivid imaginations, to give themselves the illusion they were truly flying over the waves.

After losing Rrurd and the tall cone of Kaa-meer-geh from sight, they put all their efforts into wavecrafting and windcalling, enjoying the dance up and down the mountainous waves and seeing how much they could increase their speed. The wind was southerly, forcing them to tack. If it held, it would mean a fast trip home. In the end, that was what saved Kreh-ursh's life.

How obsessed he was getting with reliving that journey! He had to get a grip. The rain had stopped, but the dripping continued. He built a mind-block against the memory, curled up on his damp bed, and tried to sleep.

Yet Kaar-oh was here! Standing in the mist outside the bivouac. Soaked to the skin. Water dripped from his hair, from his tunic, stained with wide patches of red. Then Kreh-ursh had left the shelter and was running, careering through the trees. He tripped, fell, rolled. Kaar-oh leaned down, offering his hand.

"No! Away!"

He was running again, but he knew it was useless. Again he fell, sliding downward in the dark. A night bird screeched. Something thudded against his skull, and he blacked out.

24.
STORM APPROACHING

The serpent-beast, a tower of coils, swayed above Seatown. Duu-feen had fallen, sprawled on the deck, entangled in Shahee arms and Rraawuu legs. Beside her one of Eloh-inderash's archers was aiming high at the creature's head. She struck at his arm. The arrow flew wide, sailing above the town and plopping into the lagoon. He turned, angry.

"Wait! It is a friend."

The only person standing was Taashou, legs astride, calm. Tiny as a stick doll before the monster.

"We've been waiting for you! Always the last to arrive, but ever welcome!"

Slow, ponderous, the serpent from the lightless deep looped its body back downward. Length upon length of its dripping coils slid below the waves until just the tiny head—slightly larger than Duu-feen's cabin—was hovering a few paces above the deck. Never had Duu-feen seen such an ugly sight: wrinkled skin, seaweed and barnacles growing from its scaly hide; pale eyes set wide on either side of the craggy skull, and a beardlike fringe of tentacles surrounding a cavernous mouth lined with concentric rings of serrated teeth.

Then two flaps of heavy skin on its forehead trembled and

separated. A puffy white orb was pushed forth—a blind, third eye opening. It plopped out, bouncing onto the deck and was revealed as an inflated fleh-aak-zjhur bladder. Out of the same crease squeezed a man. Climbing down the creature's face, he jumped free. On his shrill whistle, the huge creature slithered away into the lagoon, its passage sending another huge wash across the raft. The ocean returned to its rolling calm—yet not a sound came from the gathered crowd. Taashou stepped forward.

"Thank you, Daakohn, for answering my call."

Duu-feen had seen this man a few times, but never the creature he called his "boy" before. Always he had appeared from the sea, swimming. Now she knew why she had never spied his canoe. Though older than Taashou, still he stood with a youthful vigor, accentuated by his body-hugging suit of kelp. A flickering smile—he seemed childishly proud of his dramatic entrance — played about his eyes, revealing intelligence, though there was also bitterness carved into his face. He picked up the fleh-aak-zjhur bladder from the deck and methodically squeezed out the air until it was small and compact enough to attach to his belt.

"Where do you want me?"

Taashou pointed to a seat at her right hand.

Little by little people found their voices, and a hostile growl rose among the crowd as Daakohn-bhah-ehl-bhah-her walked to the spot Taashou had indicated. The mood was not pleasant: None of the land people were relaxed, not with three huge bhaanj clinging to the mainmast and a giant sea serpent cruising the depths below.

Around a hundred people sat in four main groups: Gathered around Taashou were the Shahee, the sea nomads, with Daakohn seated directly on her right; Kehl-grehnaa and her dragon riders were to her left; Gordonor and the other

Rraawuu from the city occupied the space directly facing her; and on Taashou's far left and Gordonor's right were Raa-geh-ur and his Taagaag-ee, the horse nomads of the plains; opposite them, to Taashou's right and Gordonor's left, were Eloh-inderash and his herders from the lower slopes of Geh-urbh-Geh-ot. They stabbed unfriendly looks toward Kehl-grehnaa and her companions. Cattle were one of the favorite meals of wild mountain bhaanj. Taashou stood.

"I wish to thank you, Taagaag-ee, Geyg-ee, Rraawuu, and Shahee, peoples of the land and sea, for heeding my call and agreeing to a meeting of the Great Council..."

"A call of spite... to bring us onto such a flimsy raft in this treacherous weather!" grumbled Gordonor.

She ignored him.

"I called you because of a problem that is threatening Shah, yet one that will be a danger for the whole world, should we allow it to grow. I'm talking about the rift. It has returned, yet in an evil configuration. We..."

"Taashou." It was Raa-gehd-ur. "I and my tribe are nomads like the Shahee, but nomads of the land. I have heard of this rift only in a fire myth we sing to our children but know nothing about it that I would trust as fact. Explain what you mean."

"The rift is a phenomenon that returns at irregular times, maybe once every generation or two. It is years since the last time... and I was young, just a girl... Daakohn, you should explain."

The slim, kelp-suited man stood.

"You know of me, Raa-gehd, but maybe very little. For though, like you, I grew up among the grassy plains and rode with the Taagaag-ee, I have not slept more than a night on land for over sixty years. Your father was a baby when I left, too young to remember his older brother, and the Taagaag-ee now know me simply as the Lost One."

"This family reunion is touching," snapped Gordonor, "but can we get on? I have to be back on land before nightfall. I've got a city to run!"

Daakohn laughed. "For you, Gordonor, I will keep it brief. For several generations we have known that our world and everything it contains—vast though we may see it—is like a simple bubble of sea foam born on the waves compared to the universe that surrounds it. Within this universe are many other worlds, as numerous as bubbles of sea foam…"

Duu-feen listened to Daakohn speak, but the atmosphere of the council was not the cooperative one which Taashou had hoped for. Soon Gordonor had hijacked the discussion, and was demanding to know how much payment he could expect for helping to save Shah. His mood seemed to influence the other land people.

"You, the Shahee, spend your days lazing and fishing. Now you say you need our help. Well, if you want Rraawuu aid, we might come to some more satisfying agreement on Solgom's fish supply…"

He would have continued, but a wash of wind seemed to sweep across the raft, almost as if a shadow had darkened the sky. It was no physical phenomenon but a mental one. Every person gathered on that raft who knew even the most rudimentary mind speech felt the panic in the distant mind call. It was Bel-geer, normally the calmest of shahiroh:

A black storm has been unleashed! Poison is spilling from the passage of the whirlpool, greater than before! Shah is dying…

Taashou turned to Kehl-grehnaa: "You and your bhaanj are the fleetest among us. Go, find out what has happened. I will follow as fast as I am able."

The circling bhaanj seemed to sense their riders' urgency and swooped down onto the deck. Panic erupted among the townspeople and herders, but before they could react, before a single archer could string his bow, the riders had mounted and were being lifted back up into the clouds, gliding around in an arc, and winging their way southeast. Taashou turned to the other leaders:

"Eloh-inderash, Raa-gehd-ur… Gordonor, the time has come for action yet we still have no plan. Forgive me for disrupting the council, but I must go and face this threat. If you can await my return, we will talk then. If not, I will come to each of you on land, as circumstances allow."

She turned, seeking out Duu-feen with her eyes before coming across to her.

"Wait here in Seatown." She spoke in words to avoid her thoughts being caught by others. "I must go. Organize the Shahee to support the shahiroh. Get the land people back to the mainland and return here with every canoe you can muster. Soon we will need every able-bodied person who can handle a canoe to protect Shah."

She turned and strode off in the direction of the dock, leaving Duu-feen to deal with an apoplectic Gordonor and the irate land people.

25.
THE VOLCANO

Kreh-ursh opened his eyes into a bright shaft of sunlight, head throbbing. Around him the jungle steamed as heat evaporated the previous evening's rain. Every muscle and limb complained when he rolled over and sat up. The jungle now looked innocent, clothed in bright yellow and green, no sign of ghosts, or Kaar-oh—if that had been him, the specter that had chased him in the night.

Getting to his feet, he looked around. Lost. Above, the slope climbed toward the volcano, below it dropped away to the shore. Which way was camp? He tried to remember whether he had run uphill or down, with the cone on his left or right. It was all a blank. Studying the ground for signs of his progress, he saw the place where he had slipped. That trunk there would be where he hit his head, knocked himself out. He struggled uphill, retracing his route. But then he couldn't see any more clues, his footprints were hidden by the thick humus. A short distance off, he noticed a broken branch—maybe he had passed through there. He headed in that direction.

It was late in the morning by the time he stumbled into camp, after searching and going back on his own tracks countless times. He felt more relieved than he would admit—the fear of being lost on this island with no tools, not even a knife, had gnawed at him. Flopping down on the ground in the clearing, he rested, relishing the pleasure of being surrounded by his own things: the remains of the felled tree, rough-cut timber, his bivouac, blankets, flasks, and provisions. In a short time this clearing had come to mean home. Yet the island was beginning to fray his nerves.

The only way out was to complete his task. After a while, he rose and went on with the job of planing and smoothing planks using his blades and sanding stones. Polishing and polishing until the timber began to shine, took on a mellow, burnished sheen. Throughout the long day he labored, a day of physical exercise to tire his mind. By nightfall his muscles were screaming, wracked by cramps, joints aching. Nevertheless, after dinner, even though darkness had fallen, he kept working to the light of a fire in the middle of the clearing. Only when he could no longer remain on his feet did he collapse in his bivouac, exhausted yet content with the progress made. For once, he slept soundly. If Kaar-oh reappeared, Kreh-ursh remained unaware.

The following days were spent working, taking time out just to hunt and gather the necessary food. In the middle of the clearing, a fire burned continuously. Beside it he built a tiny, tightly woven hut. He heated stones, pushed them inside, and sprinkled water over them until the hut filled with steam. He repeated this process hour after hour, passing the planks, section by section, through the steam-filled hut. In this way, he softened them. To shape them he bound them into position using strong cords, then twisted the cords tighter and tighter using a branch for a tourniquet. He rubbed juice from the acidic aank berries into the wet grain to soften the fibers further, gain more working time, so he could stretch the planks exactly how he wanted. Once the juice dried, it set the wood grain into position, harder, more resilient than before.

All this time, he refused to acknowledge Kaar-oh, though little by little the spirit had crept back into his consciousness. He was aware of him as a constant presence around the camp. It got so that when Kreh-ursh awoke, he knew Kaar-oh—his head wound constantly dripping red—would be standing at the entrance to his bivouac. If he went to check his snares, his dead friend walked beside him. While he was eating, the other boy squatted on the far side of the flames, staring, waiting for him to speak—waiting, always waiting.

"I won't leave you, you know. Even if you leave this island, I'll travel with you. I'll be part of you, Kreh-ursh, until you finally choose to see me."

Kreh-ursh was sanding the hull, Kaar-oh standing beside the bows. Almost half a moon after leaving his home, the vessel was taking shape. Kreh-ursh refused to meet his friend's eyes, keeping his own fixed on his craft. It was a very simple design: one long, straight beam was the one he chose to split, splice, and bind into the curve of a keel, which rose high at the stern into a carved post with a notch for the steering paddle. On either side of the keel, gently curved at both ends, two planks formed the lower hull, bound to the keel and to each other. Other planks, also curved, rose into the upper sides. The whole craft was bound together with tough, fibrous creepers from the jungle and wooden pins that held the planks tight. He had worked sap drawn from the shee-ou tree into the cracks. Less than a day after being tapped from the trunk, this gum set into a hard resin. By coating the boat's hull with the shee-ou sap and sanding it down when dry, using a stone wrapped in a tough piece of skur hide, the boy gave his canoe a sheen that acted like caulking and waterproofing but let it fly through the water.

All at once he decided. He met Kaar-oh's eyes:

"No, Kaar-oh, you're dead. It's over. Whatever happens, when I leave this island, you won't come."

Then he left his canoe, walked in among the trees. He didn't look back to see whether the other was following, just knew that he would. He headed up the slope. The going was tough. Both he and Kaar-oh, climbing beside him, were soon panting from the exertion. At one point, trying to pull himself up onto a log, his friend was there, reaching down a helping hand. He almost took it. Almost. Not quite. He brushed through the shade and kept climbing, climbing, climbing through the jungle.

After a sixth of a tide cycle, he began to feel thirsty

and realized his water was back at camp. He had not thought to bring any provisions, and no weapon except the knife at his belt. As he rose higher up the volcano, trees closed in. Tendrils of mist curled around their trunks. It felt chilly; though he was sweating from his climb, he barely noticed.

He had been climbing for maybe half a tide cycle—parched but relentless—when he broke through the tree line. It was sudden, with virtually no transition. For a while he had noticed the vegetation was lower, scrubbier; then he was climbing around boulders and bushes. Finally, he came out onto a large, flat rock. Before him, the bare cone rose and was lost in the amethyst twilight.

He could not continue without water, and a great height of rock still stretched above. Kaar-oh sat facing him, resting against a stone. Blood dripped from the boy's wound onto the path that Kreh-ursh must take. So close, but he knew he could not go on.

26.
TRYING TO SEE

K reh-ursh had to rest. He collapsed on the rocky slope and gazed at Kaar-oh sitting opposite him. His dead friend appeared as solid as a living being. He pondered each detail. The image was horrific. On the side of his head that the keen-skur had bitten clean away, shards of bone stuck out of the hole in his skull. Blood and brain were perpetually dripping down onto his shoulder. Kaar-oh continued to stare back until Kreh-ursh was forced to avert his eyes.

He listened hard to their surroundings. Water, he must have it… or he would faint.

"Is there any water around here, Kaar-oh?"

"Why should I tell you? You want to kill me. You killed me once, and now you want to kill me again."

"It's nature, Kaar-oh. You're dead by nature. You've got to stop, give up this world, go wherever the other spirits go… It's probably better there, anyway."

Kaar-oh looked out into the mist. Kreh-ursh followed his gaze and realized that he could see through the dense haze. He was looking out over the sea of Shah. Islands dotted the vast expanse. Beyond, he saw Kaa-meer-geh nestled close to the bay of Rrurd and the mainland. Yet it should be impossible to see so far. He could see Gaa-shuudot River toward the south, and even the place where they had moored the canoe, where Kaar-oh had died. Kreh-ursh looked even farther, across the mainland, saw the flats, forest, desert, hills, and, far away on the horizon, two tiny mountains— one a little higher than the other: Geh-urbh-Geh-ot, where it was said all creation had begun.

Kaar-oh sighed. "I'll never let go of life, Kreh-ursh. I love it too much. It's… This world is so much a part of me…" He was silent for a good while, then: "I wanted to be a Shahee… It's not fair that you are completing sea-nomad-becoming and I cannot… The keen-skur's fang was your idea!"

Kreh-ursh did not know what to say. How could he destroy Kaar-oh's talisman now? That was what he had decided to do, and Kaar-oh knew. To take the bag with his amulet up to the volcano's crater and throw it in, watch it burn. Surely Kaar-oh would be forced to move on then, to go wherever he had to go?

Kaar-oh nodded downhill a short way to the right.

"There's a stream just there. You can drink."

And there was. Kreh-ursh could now hear it trickling. Why hadn't he heard it before? He walked tiredly downhill and quenched his thirst. Night had almost fallen by the time they arrived back at camp.

It took Kreh-ursh several days to carve his protection symbols onto the stern post and gouge out two eyes on either side of the prow so his vessel could "see" where she was going. Over the following days, he shaped the largest branches cast aside from the crown. Of two long, curving boughs, he fashioned outrigger arms. With three thin, straight limbs, he prepared a tripod-style mast for the gaff. He did not attach those but placed them inside the canoe for his journey down to the sea. He also carved himself a paddle from a piece of wide, flat wood.

That night, maybe because he was feeling exhilarated as his vessel neared completion, he fell asleep quickly. No dreams.

The next morning, as he was scouting down the slope for the easiest passage to the stream, he made a decision. He was studying a shallow channel, hardly more than a depression, leading down and slightly to the right and Kaar-oh was speaking, as if in the back of his mind, giving his opinion on which route Kreh-ursh should choose. Kreh-ursh was on the point of answering him angrily, telling him to shut up—this was his sea-nomad-becoming. Then he remembered that Kaar-oh was dead. Was he going mad? How was it that he had assimilated Kaar-oh so far into himself? With a wrench, he ripped the other's talisman from his breast and threw it behind him, not looking to see where it landed.

Then he hurled himself into the job of moving his canoe. He placed chopped-up branches as rollers, chose his route, and began to drag the craft downhill. A third of a tide-cycle, at least, it took him, to reach the stream;

then he left the boat on the bank and walked back up to his campsite to gather his belongings and supplies.

Kaar-oh stood there, half hidden in the trees.

"You've chosen wrongly, Kreh-ursh. That won't help you. Why do you hate me so much?"

Blocking out Kaar-oh's presence, Kreh-ursh began to gather his gear, taking a hurried look around the clearing. So long, so many days that this had been home, and here he was running like a coward, but he had to get out of this forest. It was driving him crazy. He needed the ocean about him; it was his blood. Maybe that was why Kaar-oh had found it so easy to take hold. Besides, all the time he'd been here, he'd been hungry, to the point that he no longer really noticed hunger except as a stronger or weaker sensation of pain in his belly. True, the island boasted abundant resources, but his energy had been focused only on completing sea-nomad-becoming, so he had spent little time hunting and gathering.

He noticed how scarce liquid remained in his flask. He must save the rest for the return journey. He would fill the flask with water from the stream, diluting the potion but eking out its power over several more days. Kaar-oh made a move toward him. Kreh-ursh turned away, but not before he'd caught the flash of anger on the boy's face. He would not look, would not acknowledge him. He walked away downhill, leaving his friend's ghost abandoned among the trees.

27.
THE BIRTH OF KREH-OTCHAW-OH

Kreh-ursh heaved his canoe down the muddy bank and into the stream. Seeming still to feel Kaar-oh's presence at his shoulders, nevertheless he would not turn back. Though glad to be rid of the amulet—it had been a source of torment since first he came onto the island—the stream blurred in his eyesight.

He relived that terrible moment afresh: The keen-skur had set up a violent rocking, writhing its coiled body in the water under the canoe. Kaar-oh should not have stood up, but he was trying to raise the sail to blow them to safety. Then the keen-skur leapt—even as Kaar-oh fell backward out of the canoe—up it flew, closing its jaws around his skull, crushing the bone like eggshell, bursting Kaar-oh's short life from him in an instant. Kreh-ursh stretched out to grab him, but his scarlet amulet pouch was the only thing that came away in his hand, that talisman bag with the broken cord. A hideous shower of blood drenched the canoe, staining the water scarlet, drawing in predators. And Kreh-ursh was spinning the vessel on its course, away from the keen-skur's lair—the water churned red, chunks of flesh floating on the surface, snapped up quickly by unseen creatures. The sail tripod rested lopsidedly across the outrigger, just a half-hearted flap catching the breeze—nothing else to contact the elements, both paddles having been wrenched from their hands, crunched and broken in the gnashing teeth. Yet a chant was coursing from Kreh-ursh's throat—hardly was he aware of knowing the forms so intuitively—and the canoe was flying across the waves, back toward Rrurd and safety, Rrurd and his family.

All this flashed through Kreh-ursh's mind as he stumbled along beside his canoe. The water, knee deep, splashed him, and he again seemed to feel the stickiness of that blood-splattered canoe under his touch as he fled the site of his friend's death.

Kaar-oh's figure floated along the bank, not approaching, but never leaving. He seemed to be asking, wanting something. Kreh-ursh kept his head down, trying to focus only on the splashing water around his legs. Yet still he heard the thought:

You can't run from me, you know, you'll have to return. I could have helped you... have helped you... I can go where you can't. Remember me... where you are going... Remember the one of far touch.

The next time Kreh-ursh raised his head, the bloody vision of his former friend had drifted or faded back into the jungle. Kreh-ursh felt suddenly alone. He realized he was trembling, his body soaked in sweat while a chill washed over him. Kaar-oh must have turned back to stay near his amulet. Kreh-ursh continued downstream, pushing his canoe.

The journey was both easy and difficult. Using a

moving chant—one created for dragging fishnets or paddling over long distances, he eased his vessel forward. At stages they traveled quickly, the canoe half floating, half slithering over muddy banks. At other times, the vessel snagged on underwater roots, weeds, and uneven hollows in the streambed. Or else the torrent fell steeply between sheer banks. He had to maneuver carefully over many waterfalls or pull the canoe from the water and heave it overland. Sometimes sharp bends appeared, where he had to be careful not to jam the craft in the narrow channel or capsize it and see his few possessions slip away downstream.

Finally, however, they hit the flat shores of the island where the stream widened and meandered down into a small lagoon. This was a different beach from where Kreh-ursh had set off. He calculated that he had journeyed almost a quarter of the way around the volcano's cone in his search for his tree. As he waded through the shallows, guiding his craft beside him, he studied the beach cautiously, wary of who, or what, he might meet. Yet it looked empty. He made camp beside the lagoon.

That afternoon and the next day he spent on the final preparations for his journey. Binding the outrigger firmly in place so the craft was properly balanced took some time. He dove around the reef for lee-aandeh seaweed strings and used them as rigging for the tripod mast and the gaff of the sail, so he could raise and lower it quickly when needed. It took him a full day to repair, tighten, and strengthen the cheg-muug sail—the traditional triangular sail of his people—after the battering it had taken serving as his bivouac roof. Now, though, the kaank leaves were dry and light. It would work well.

Then came that moment of bursting pride: His craft was ready but for a last significant act. The ceremony was simple, as simple as carving the traditional letters into the hull behind the boat's eyes. In naming her, he chose Kreh-otchaw-oh, which meant "wavecrafter," wavecrafting being one of the five skills a full Shahee must master. She seemed to sit on the beach smiling at him, her fine, polished wood glowing golden in the relaxed rays of the early evening sun.

The following dawn, Kreh-ursh took a carefully prepared bhayd stake from his gear, along with some keerr heather bark he'd been drying for days. In a sheltered lee of the lagoon, he produced fire using the traditional method. This was the final rite, bringing fire home to his hearth at Rrurd. He opened a small earthenware pot given him by his father. Lined with charcoal and containing downward-facing air vents, if carefully protected during an ocean voyage, this pot could keep embers smoldering for days on the return journey. He waited until he had a strongly glowing bed of embers, and then shovelled some into the pot, replaced the lid, and stored it carefully in the canoe.

Then, the best part of a silver moon since he had set out from home, Kreh-ursh dragged Kreh-otchaw-oh down the beach and out into the waters of the lagoon to begin the final leg of sea-nomad-becoming—sailing home.

28.
CURRENT READING

They crossed the reef. Kreh-otchaw-oh shuddered as she crashed into, and through, the foam curtain, bracing her fresh timbers against the first ocean swells of her brief lifetime. Kreh-ursh held his breath. Would she hold up, or be smashed into driftwood? The job of paddling this tiny vessel, so small compared to the great canoe, alone into the majesty and savagery of the open sea, had been too scary to think about while he sat on the beach earlier, gazing out at that palisade of crashing spray. Yet as he trickled sand, grain by grain, through his fingers—thoughts skipping out over the lagoon toward the reef, then westward across the ocean—the solution, like a seabird alighting on the waves, settled into his mind:

You hold the answer inside yourself.

He slipped down into trance, the state used for memorizing information in class. The long days, the tiresome repetition returned, and he felt knowledge touch his mind as lightly as the sand slid off his fingertips. Kaar-oh, Geh-meer, and the others sat together; enduring the monotony of training before embarking on sea-nomad-becoming; going over and over the same chants, codes, and thought techniques, the repetitively drilled focus points. He recalled wave forms—fish-scale pattern, feather effect, choppy wave-tops against wind. Every aspect of the constantly changing sea meant something, could be interpreted if you knew how to read it. Deer-ot, their teacher, seemingly grudging with even the simplest information, would sometimes make an enigmatic statement they might not quite understand concerning the shape of a cloud, or suddenly give emphatic instructions that would make no sense at all until one day, out on the ocean, they could see and feel it, as clearly as the wind ruffles your skin. It was like learning to breathe all over again. You had to breathe the sea, know Shah like you knew your own canoe. But she was changeable, unforgiving. Learn the lesson well the first time around. You might not get another chance.

In his mind, Kreh-ursh plotted, stage by careful stage, the chants he would need to cross the reef, plus his entire course back to Rrurd. Sitting there on the beach, he also remembered nighttime visions from the island as if they were dreams, dreams in which Taashou the shahiroh appeared.

That was the whole point of sea-nomad-becoming, the reason for isolation on Zjhuud-geh, for Taashou appearing in the night, challenging him in the arena of his own mind. Passive knowledge was not enough.

To be Shahee you had to use it, know how to wield it. That was the only way of serving Shah. Sitting there on the sand, the days of hard work, the nights fighting his phantoms made sense.

He now saw how brainless his and Kaar-oh's expedition to Gaa-shuudot had been, a silly children's adventure. Kaar-oh had died because of their own idiocy. They had never known what they needed to be successful; they had only thought they did. It made him weep as he finally accepted it—Kaar-oh's death was a weight he would carry now throughout his life.

Opening his eyes wide, gazing at the jumping surf separating ocean from lagoon, he had felt ready. Ready to sail back to Rrurd, knowing what it was to be Shahee—such a different idea to what he had thought before! A Shahee was a sailor and a fisherman, but far more. The Shahee were Shah's guardians. No Shahee had the right to take from the sea except for his or her own survival. Before allowing Shah to be damaged, he must perish himself—for all creatures were just links in the ocean's single continuous chain.

Kreh-otchaw-oh hauled herself up the wide, blue back of the first ocean roller. Kreh-ursh was sweating, his paddle driving hard into the wave's surface. His voice lifted above the roar to call out the sacred syllables that bound him and his craft to the elements. They reached the top of the first wave and floated for a moment, seemingly still, on its crest. Out to the east, the sun had risen over the stretched belly of the world. Below its light, on the sparkling horizon, he saw a silhouette. It was the great canoe, rocking up and down on the ocean, its crew attentive to the candidates setting out, over these days, to make the return journey to their village in the west. He raised his paddle in salute and was answered, in the distance, by two or three raised oars. Then he sliced down into the hide of the wave. Kreh-otchaw-oh jumped and sprang, skimming fast down the green hillside, and they galloped away, seeking to circle the island and sail west.

When his back felt like it was about to break and his arms were ready to drop off, but now on a steady course due west, he rested his paddle and raised the tripod with its woven sail. The wind filled it and began to whisk them along. He tied his paddle to the stern post, using it as a rudder. Looking around at sea and sky, reading the wave formations, comparing them to the sun, he found and checked his position in relation to the piled clouds—which indicated land masses still out of sight under the horizon.

With each glance back, from the crest of each breaker, Zjhuud-geh's cone gradually shrank. Finally, the only remaining sign of the volcano was a puff of silver cloud on the horizon behind. Then even that dropped below the sea, and they were alone with nothing but blue on all sides and fresh spray on the breeze. Hot sun bathed his face after too long living in the jungle's gloom. Below he watched sparkling shoals of kree-eh turning all the colors of the rainbow, deep in the cool water. Now that they had left, even though the salt air was invigorating in his nostrils, he missed the island's rich perfume, wished he had brought some token as a present for his people. Relaxed, almost sad, he thought it strange that after his torturous ordeal, sea-nomad-becoming should be ending on such a pleasant note: this leisurely amble up and down Shah's great peaks, under a clear blue sky and a warm sun. While one eye remained open to keep their course true, Kreh-ursh slid into a contented daydream. He recalled other sailing trips: boat races up and down the coast of his village in his father's canoe, sheltered by Kaa-meer-geh's dark, reddish bulk to the northeast; lazy days fishing with friends in the quiet northern bay, their canoes bound together into a single raft, so that when they became bored with fishing they would take turns diving off into the sun-hot muddy water, one of them always keeping a lookout for the gaashaw-skur—a venomous water serpent that paralyzed with a single bite and dragged you down to its nest in the reed roots.

Kreh-ursh's head dropped back against Kreh-otchaw-oh's stern post. He slept. The paddle, hooked into its thong on the gunwale, began to flap…

A loud roaring awoke him. Instantly, he was alert and struggling with the rudder oar. Bearing down from the north, a hissing wall of foam charged toward them.

29.
SQUALL

Kreh-ursh gouged his paddle deep into the wave's back, calling on the elements under his influence. To heave Kreh-otchaw-oh around was their only hope: to run before, not meet the squall side on. If they could…

Then the shock of it hit. Wind roared. Volleys of hail hit the canoe like stones. Kreh-otchaw-oh's sail was torn from its ties by the blast. Lunging, Kreh-ursh grabbed it just as it was swept away, dragging rigging and spars behind. But the sail lifted, and pulled him bodily from the canoe. By luck, as he plunged into the water, one arm curled tight around the outrigger. With his other hand, he gripped the woven sail, refusing to let it drag him under. Pulled downward by the waterlogged matting, Kreh-otchaw-oh skidded sideways into a trough. Clinging to the outrigger, desperate to keep his head above water, Kreh-ursh mouthed a moving chant—trying to lighten the underwater weight. But his words were whipped from between his teeth as sea and hail lashed his face. He had to let the sail go. Yet in the moment of that thought, he found he couldn't—his wrist was tangled in the stays. He tightened his grip on the outrigger, knowing that letting go now was death. The canoe foundered into the wave trough, a boiling maelstrom of furious surf.

His chant strengthened. Slowly Kreh-otchaw-oh rose, keeping her gunwales above the angry sea. Shoulders aching, Kreh-ursh hauled on the sail with his free arm and pulled it from the depths. Then they were rising. Wind and rain pushed them up the side of the next wave. Kreh-ursh worked his way around to the stern of his craft, untangled his wrist from the rigging, and lashed the sail to the stern post. Finally, with what felt like the last of his strength, he heaved himself up and tumbled aboard. The sail splayed out in the water behind, acting as a sea anchor, holding their stern toward the storm.

The canoe was full of water, submerged nearly to her gunwales. As the squall thrashed them like seaweed thrown onto the beach, Kreh-ursh began to bail with one hand while battling to steer with the other, fighting the current to keep them planing downwind.

He should have been alert, ready for this danger. Squalls of this kind—half waterspout, half gale—were common on Shah. All they could do now was run south, abandoning their original course, and try to stay afloat till it was all over. Rain still lashed his back and shoulders. Kreh-otchaw-oh rode low, sluggish to respond. It seemed as if they were fighting the weather for days, beyond exhaustion. Kreh-ursh kept on bailing.

Then, as quickly as it appeared, the squall rushed past. Kreh-otchaw-oh seemed to breathe a sigh of relief, shuddering, nearly human, flapping a loose stay in farewell. With double-handed scoops and then grabbing a small bowl from his belongings, Kreh-ursh continued emptying water from the craft. Regaining buoyancy might be the key to his survival. After he had emptied about half the water, he hoisted the spars, pulled the sail back on board and hung it, letting it flap loose to dry out.

He kept bailing. Soon most of the water was gone. He pulled in the sheet and adjusted their course due west. From now on, he would have to keep a better lookout. In this tiny craft, he could not afford to sleep until he reached land. He had no idea how far off course they might be. Furthermore, with this overcast sky, these confused wave patterns did not help to pinpoint their position. However, any bearing due west would at least bring them to land, hopefully no further south than the great river. Then they could sail up the coast to Rrurd.

The wide hills and valleys of the ocean rose and fell as before, an unbroken, green expanse. He was emptying the last few finger widths of water from the canoe when a patch of crimson in the bottom caught his eye. Something caught underneath the twig matting on the bottom floated free. He picked it up, heart thudding against his ribcage. This should not be here! But as he stretched his arm back to hurl it out into the wide ocean, something checked him. He curled his fist around the scarlet bag. How could it have ended up here? He threw it away on the island! Kaar-oh and his talisman should have stayed there, on Zjhuud-geh! He couldn't fathom how… unless when he threw it… could it have landed by some improbable chance…? Kaar-oh must have interfered somehow. Was that possible? He was a spirit, nonexistent; he lacked substance. How could he possibly…? Kreh-ursh tucked the bag among his belongings and spat into the water.

The hint of sun visible through the clouds showed it was almost midday. He had no idea how long this voyage would last. Might he reach land that day, as fast as the great canoe that brought him to Zjhuud-geh? He doubted it. He would be sailing by starlight— for one or several nights. The cloud patterns, now he paid attention, were odd—nothing he recognized from training—as if the entire sky were cloaked in silver fish scales, yet with an uncanny, circular movement in the upper hemisphere he could not remember ever having seen. It was as if an enormous paddle had been dug into the clouds and was gouging a swirling pattern into their substance, a giant whirlpool forming in the sky…

It would be good to get home. For so long, the only company he'd had were Taashou and Kaar-oh—if you could call them company, a witch and a dead boy. Taashou alone would have been preferable. Nor had he met any other candidate since Geh-meer had helped him with the dragon—they would keep that a secret. He felt lonely, had seen no sign of the great canoe since that brief glimpse off the sacred island. It felt as if he were the sole person on the sea. Alone—alone throughout the entire crossing from island to mainland. Shah, the wide ocean, stretched away on all sides, the only break that odd patch of brown farther to the south.

It looked familiar.

30.
PINE BLUFF

Jade was not sure where she was headed, just needed to get out after dinner and walk. Her feet led her down the road. Joan had been on the phone most of the time while cooking dinner—fried liver as hard as a ship's biscuit, flaky potatoes, gray peas—scribbling notes furiously onto a legal pad. A friend from Wild Watch had called—that was when she had rubberized the carrots—to tell her he had "accessed" the Port Authority database. She began to take notes: shipping company, vessel, ports of departure and destination, dates, cargoes... There were seven companies with ships passing within five miles of the coast... two ships carrying oil or oil products.

"Listen to this..." Joan propped open a thick legal volume on the defrosting packet of peas she had forgotten to put back in the freezer: "'Where a harbor master has reason to believe that the ship owner has committed an offence under Section 131 by the discharge from the ship of oil into harbor waters, the harbor master may detain...' Yes, but we're talking about the open sea..."

Too late, Jade caught a whiff of burnt onions.

"But you say they have all the permits? So there's really no evidence..."

Jade scraped crisp, black bits onto her plate, thinking that she really must learn to cook.

"...but Section 284... 'In its application to the detention of a vessel under this section, shall have effect with the omission of subsections (1), (6), and (7) and... in (a) subsection (2), the reference to "competent authority" being a reference to the harbor authority; and (b) in subsection (4), persons in relation to whom that subsection applies...' We still need to show that the slick came from that particular vessel... that they're polluting the bay... It comes down again to the fact we have no proof..."

Jade always found she could think better when surrounded by her favorite sliding sandscape. Out of sight of the house, she stepped into the dunes, walking northward toward Pine Bluff. Her mom would give her a hiding if she knew: *Don't leave the track—you'll wreck the ecosystem!* She wandered toward the shore. Here the ground was sandy, straggling pines growing down to the water, their roots bracing the sandy soil. The bank shelved steeply—not really a bluff, but it was what everybody called it—the place below where the Mauri River emptied into the bay, river and ocean currents colliding in a violent choppiness.

The jetty road ended in an open area fifty yards beyond, but Jade sat down under trees close to the bank. The tussling water brought up thoughts of Kyle as he was yesterday, battling the waves on his oversized boogie board. How life could change in a day! She had failed her brother, and to make matters worse she seemed to be losing her mind. Why? Something to do with her dream? Things were about to change, she knew, but did not know how, just had a feeling of horror deep in her bones, maybe like the way animals can sense an earthquake hours before it happens. There must be some relation between it all… but what? All of these things, the laughter and ominous moaning, the clouds, her dream, and always the desire to drop down, farther down into the deep, to dive into the green…

…hurzjh-faadaw-oh…

That mocking laughter seemed to be saying… *What? Try as hard as you can, you'll never understand.* The language of those guttural syllables. It was tiring to think about any of it.

She heard someone coming toward the bank. She didn't really feel like speaking to anyone in the mood she was in and was about to move farther along when she caught a flash of blue serge. She looked around. Several yards away, two pines had collapsed together. A third leaned in over them at an angle. Where the trunks met they formed a kind of teepee, buried under sand. Underneath was a hollow just large enough to squeeze into. She hid. From there she could look out between cracks in the trunks.

The footsteps came right up to the teepee. She held her breath, watching the intruder's feet—black leather shoes, formal trousers of navy serge with a thin white stripe down the outside. Yes, she definitely knew that uniform. The legs bent at the knees as the newcomer squatted down, and Jade pressed herself deeper into the hollow. Then pale stony eyes and a mass of dirty blond hair came into sight: Rena, dressed for work. She was staring at the hollow but amazingly did not see Jade. She lit a cigarette and began to smoke it. Sometimes she looked toward Jade's hiding place, but in a slightly bored way, staring without seeing, like you would gaze out of the classroom window during a boring class on a beautiful day.

Jade didn't dare breathe. She was finished if Rena discovered her. There they were, alone together, miles from anyone who might have saved her. Rena stood up and walked over to the group of pines. She sat down on one of the trunks. Now all Jade could see was one wide blue thigh blocking a narrow crack between the trunks. Rena farted. What had Jade done to deserve this? She could barely control herself, just knew that she must. If Rena discovered her, she would be history.

31. DEATH ISLAND

With one watchful eye on the horizon—he could not afford to be caught by another squall—Kreh-ursh studied the patch of brown as it drifted closer. Maybe it was one of those floating weed islands brimming with vegetation, even wildlife—just like a real island—that occasionally appeared on Shah.

The weather was picking up, claiming more of his attention, the wind rising, pushing Kreh-otchaw-oh along faster. The breeze was southerly, allowing them a fast tack westward. He reefed in further. Kreh-otchaw-oh's sail and rigging functioned but needed more work. She was maneuvering too sluggishly.

Soon, he realized he would pass close by the dark shape, which had now become a wide mass extending over a large stretch of water. Not a floating island, he hoped it was nothing that might foul Kreh-otchaw-oh's hull. If he could just tack past, allowing a safe margin on its north side. He reefed Kreh-otchaw-oh in tighter, so she began to lean over to the side, her outrigger rising from the water as the wind swelled her sail into a pregnant crescent moon. He grabbed a spare pole that was stored in the bottom of the boat and bound it tightly to the handle of his paddle, which was attached securely to the stern as a rudder. By holding the end of the pole at arm's length, he was able to stack out over the water and could still work the rudder.

The brown mass came closer. Its glistening surface hugged the waves, smoothing and rounding them, rolling and sliding thickly on the ocean's back. He would have to pass within several canoe lengths of it. It was dark, flickering with rainbow reflections, and sluggishly fluid—like mud. Soon he noticed that its surface was pricked by bumps, odd protrusions, shapes like small hillocks, even bushes or bare branches sprouting from the mass. It looked almost like a dead forest, gradually rotting, decaying in primeval slime. And the smell was hideous.

Then he saw movement. A shape fluttered. He gasped. He recognized that creature. His stomach turned over. Still alive, trapped in the stinking slime, it struggled to stay above water. Feebly it strained upward, thrashing sodden wings, shrieking to escape. As he watched, it made a last leap upwards. *Ssccrreeeaaaggghhhh!!* Its call was shredded on the ocean breeze. Then it was swallowed below the surface, not to rise again.

His canoe surged past at a few boat-lengths' distance. Now horrified, he saw other creatures trapped in the muck, floating half dead or lifeless: a family of rruush-oh stranded on the surface like a colony of oversized mushrooms, their fine, silver parachutes stained a poisonous brown, flapping emptily in the wind; a Shah-skur lying dead across the surface, its elegant, acrobatic coils reduced to one lank S-shape, its scales like broken brown teeth. The dark sludge was a graveyard for all the sea's life, creatures from above and below the surface trapped and killed in its clutch.

Kreh-ursh felt sick. From where had this island of death appeared? He was chilled numb, sitting there in his boat, yet anger burned deep down. It began to form at the base of his gut while the wasted wildlife slid by, a dull sheen of death staring out from lifeless eyes.

He swore revenge. He would redeem each and every death he saw here, find the cause, and destroy it—even if it took a lifetime. Was this why he wanted to become Shahee? Was this what he must face? Confronting such horrors, healing such ravages: It looked a far bleaker future than he had imagined. Despair coated the cold iron of his anger, but the rage remained huge.

Kreh-otchaw-oh cleared the death slick, and then the clouds once more opened and it began to pelt down. The wind dropped. Within moments he could see little but rain driving in sheets across the sea. Kreh-otchaw-oh was thrown up and down on the swells. The ocean turned black, wave crests flashing silver. Lightning struck from the sky, followed by a long, rolling peal of thunder. Kreh-ursh began to get nervous. A bolt might strike the highest point in the surrounding area in its effort to reach the earth. Right now, sitting in a canoe in the middle of the ocean, he was the highest point around. He lowered the mast, covered the open boat with the sail, and crouched inside, concentrating on just keeping his craft end-on to the high, choppy waves that buffeted them. The air had turned chill. Soon he was shivering. He wrapped himself in his sleeping mat, trying to keep warm.

Suddenly, lightning flashed, and he gasped. Believing he had been alone on the empty sea mere moments before, he felt his heart stop: Another craft was outlined in the blue light. The unknown canoe was closing fast. Black and rain-lashed, it crested the next high wave and dropped swiftly down the wave's slope toward him.

32.
DUSK RENDEZVOUS

Rena's farts pummeled Jade like a raging storm, the poisonous gas leaching down between the tree trunks. An analysis of the odors coming from the older girl's bowels suggested that whoever cooked for her had even less skill than Jade's mom. The main ingredients seemed to be burnt garlic and an element that could only be rotting, barbecued rat.

Then the whine of a dune buggy filtered through the trees. Rena got up, and a tiny amount of fresh air wafted in. Jade gasped. The engine roar lurched closer until a large rubber tire skidded to a halt nearby.

"You took your time, Screwie. We said seven."

The drawling voice that answered Rena was one Jade recognized: "Relax, he isn't here yet. So what's the problem?"

"Got any beer?"

"Security staff shouldn't drink on duty. Here."

Jade heard first one can pop open, then another. Screwdriver sat on the buggy tire. A moment later there was a *thunk!* that sounded far too close for comfort. Turning her head slightly, she saw a worn screwdriver, its blade sharpened to a vicious point, quivering beside her ear like an arrow in the tree trunk. A hairy forearm passed close beside her face to retrieve it. Seconds later, another *thunk* sounded, and the screwdriver again landed in the wood. Jade was now thinking wistfully of Rena's farts. With Screwdriver there, she had managed to control her hardworking bowels, but Jade would happily have had that foul stink instead of Screwdriver's amateur knife act. She prayed, as the blade *thunked* a third time into the trunk, that Screwdriver had been practicing hard.

From away under the pines came a loud grunt and crash, as if someone had walked into a tree. It interrupted Screwdriver's knife-throwing act.

"The Head."

"I can hear a car, too. That has to be him. Hurry up, Head!"

An older boy the size and shape of a brick outhouse stumbled up through the trees.

"Sorry, guys. I got lost. Did you see me walk bang smack into that tree? Broad daylight and everything! I was looking the wrong way."

So now they had an entire reunion… of the Adams family. Maybe they called him the Head because of how his shoulders sloped straight up into his hairline with no visible neck, so the upper half of his body looked all head. Then again the name could be ironic, as he was not renowned in Mauri Cove for being an intellectual giant. Jade suspected Rena had picked him for his unquestioning loyalty.

"Just in time—he's here already."

The quiet purr of an engine could be heard gliding down the jetty road.

"Okay, Head. Remember—keep your lips shut, even if he speaks to you directly. I'll do the talking."

Rena shot her empty can with some misplaced instinct right into the hole where Jade was hiding, hard enough to leave her face bruised for a week. Screwdriver copied her, but there was a clunk. Rena howled.

"Gee—sorry, girl. I missed."

Tires crunched to a halt on the jetty road. A car door clicked, and footsteps approached. The gang of three walked to meet the new arrival. Taking advantage of their absence, Jade stretched cramped muscles, craned her neck slightly, and peered out to see who it was. The figure who entered the clearing, squat in a gray suit, was Dr. Hagues, CEO of Synengine Energies, Inc.

33.
MEETING AT SEA

Before Kreh-ursh had time to react, the dark canoe had coasted down the wave with an eerie swiftness and was alongside. Taashou grabbed his craft, and bound it to hers. She had abandoned her ceremonial mask, was dressed in a plain gray shift under her blue cloak, soaking hair tied tight behind her neck. Rain and spray had drenched her completely, but she appeared impervious, allowing the water to lash her face and body as if numb to the cold. She scrambled into his canoe. He stared in shock. How did she find him, alone in a tiny boat in the ocean in the middle of a storm? But she was not there for social conversation:

Kreh-ursh! Her eyes bored into him as her mind hit his with more intensity than he had ever felt. *The Death. Did you see it?*

Before he was able to speak, she had answered her own question, plucking the death island image from his mind like a flower off a plant, examining it, and tossing it aside. Then she had no more use for words, no time. Her mind opened—he felt it like a busy network of tunnels diverging, curving, and joining before him—and drew him in. Possibilities stemmed like passages to each side, above, below. Yet as if in a dream where you struggled to advance, he could not move freely. She prodded his mind, not so much inviting as herding his consciousness into her mental space, directing him toward a particular zone. While rain lashed his face and his limbs trembled, he remained oblivious to the storm's violence, falling deep into the shahiroh's inner world.

Below, he saw a land arrayed in all its length and breadth. His own. Geh-urbh-Geh-ot's twin peaks formed a center point; around them swirled mountain ranges, hills, forests, deserts, and grasslands. Shah, the wide sea, stretched blue-green to the east, dotted with single islands and speckled archipelagos.

In a rush Kreh-ursh and Taashou, like birds, zoomed in toward the volcano island of Kaa-meer-geh, saw a gathering—the shahiroh. This was the second time he had been treated to a vision of the red rock isle where the shahiroh lived. What did this all mean? The blue-robed figures were intent on a task. He could not see as much as feel the force of their minds gathered, focused on a single objective.

Images rose toward him as Taashou let him view more. Again he saw the death island rolling over the sea, sucking creatures to their doom as it floated menacingly along. Then the island was gone, and he was rushed into another vision—a desert. This barren tract was recent, the result of a great drying out—trees and greenery had been starved, killed; the sky was pale, the color of bleached bone. He could not see what was causing it—the damage—but he saw dying animals, trees withering, drought reaching out its grasping fingers. Somehow the water had been sucked away.

The vision changed, and he saw more mountains, as in his previous vision of Geh-urbh-Geh-ot. Yet here were many more, a whole land made of shining snow and ice: the most beautiful sight he had ever seen— harsh and violent yet pure and untouched as a primeval dawn. Though this land, too, was changing, withering. It was cracking, breaking up into pieces, dying. The sky sucked in poison, and the landscape melted. The vision stretched to include the whole world, and now storms raged across its face. Deserts were sucked up by tornadoes and thrown like blankets across entire forests, smothering them. People in villages and towns died from disease and poisoning. Others watched from high land as their homes were flooded by rising tides. Still others starved as their crops withered and failed, sometimes poisoned, sometimes destroyed by drought or flood.

Then that door shut on him, and he was pushed farther into the labyrinth.

He was in space, bodiless, in a perception of reality he had never known. He felt Taashou's mind next to his, within his and around, conscious of how they linked. The two of them formed part of a wide net, like a fishing net, but including everything imaginable within it. Other worlds were there, too, stretching out into endless space, but meanwhile contained within each other, like an infinity of baskets, one placed inside the other, intermeshed and interwoven in a way he could conceive but not picture—yet each replete in its own capsule of time.

Then he saw, sensed, a link, where one world seemed momentarily to brush another in time and space. It formed like a tunnel or bridge, a gossamer spider's thread linking the two dimensions. They opened, united, were briefly one. Their substance flowed together, each feeding the other, as though the separate realities were fertilizing, pollinating each other for a time before the link snapped and the two universes parted again, became individual bubbles, isolated yet connected within the same ocean.

The rift.

This was the rift, her mind speech informed him. He saw the bridge form again, between two other unknown worlds. And again. Each time, the worlds seemed to brush. There was a point of contact. Out stretched the gossamer tornado bridge, and those worlds communed with each other for a spell before contact was broken. Focusing again on his own world, he saw the bridge linking them with another place— and now he sensed that sickness, a basic imbalance affecting his own world, flowing in from outside. And matter—his ocean replete with its kree-eh shoals— being sucked out. The source was that foreign world, yet all worlds were connected. The rot, he knew, was now part of his own.

34.
DR. HAGUES

Rena's gang towered over Dr. Hagues. As if to give himself the advantage, he walked straight up to the group of trunks where Jade was hiding before turning to face them. Though scant yards away, Jade had to strain to catch what he said. Hagues barely raised his voice above a whisper.

"I'm glad you could come, Rena, lads."

"I wa…" the Head began, but Rena cuffed him, and he was silent.

She spoke instead: "We're here to help you out, sir."

"Do you kids know why we chose to build our laboratory here at Point Mauri?"

"We are so grateful for that, Dr. Hagues, your company taking the initiative of bringing work into the area… lowering unemployment…"

"Yes, yes, naturally. But that isn't the reason. This area is swarming with environmental groups… Only a very dimwitted businessman would dream of setting up here. But look out there."

They looked, as did Jade.

"It's that current, the river mouth and ocean current… so perfect for our needs."

"What you explained the other day, Dr. Hagues—that's certainly ingenious, how you've managed to calculate the risks and can keep our area so clean and picturesque. The greenies certainly can't argue with that."

The two boys nodded. When the Head went to speak, Screwdriver pricked him with his weapon.

"And beyond, what do you see?"

"Ah, the sea?"

"Yes. That marvelous, never-ending, barely touched resource. But something else."

"I can't see anything," growled Rena. Jade could tell she was rapidly losing patience with Hagues' enigmatic approach.

"Out there, where you can't see anything, are certain coordinates, which I discovered many years ago…"

"Didn't know you'd been to Mauri Cove before, sir."

"I haven't. I'm not really a biologist, you know, more of a physicist. Those coordinates make this the best spot for my enterprise."

Rena's eyes lit up. "You don't mean the research station out there, do you?"

"I do. Do you see that storm brewing out there, kids?"

"Of course, sir."

Dr. Hagues laughed. "Well, I created that!"

All three, along with Jade in her hiding spot, were shocked.

"That storm is going to make me extremely rich. It could make you kids rich into the bargain. If you stick by me."

"We're with you, sir," said Rena, and the other two nodded.

"In these early stages, it's all a bit messy. Eventually, we'll get a pipeline in—much cleaner—but until then, you remember your job. Keep people away. If you think there's the slightest suspicion…"

"I understand, sir—we call it off."

"Don't be dim! I have far too much money invested in this. Just do whatever you need to keep snoopers away. Both from the river and the research station. Outage is at seven next morning—it's tricky, but we need to use the tides. And we can't afford to have any early morning anglers mucking up my plans."

Dr. Hagues took a bunch of keys from his pocket, slipped an L-shaped tool from the ring, and passed it to Rena.

"You're the only one I want in my lab… Understand? Your buddies' job is to keep that river clean… No fishermen, nothing. Use the launch we use for the harvest. It's powerful… straight from the showroom. So I don't want it knocked about. Remember, I'm paying you for absolute discretion. Report to me in the morning, once outage is done."

He left them, walking with quick steps back to his car. They were silent until his car purred into life and cruised away up the jetty road. Jade remained mystified. She waited. Yet it was only as they were jumping into their buggy that Rena said, "You guys be on the river by five, okay? Outage: seven. Give it a couple of hours to flow down the river. The tide turns at eight-thirty and should wash it all out. Problem solved. But keep people away till at least twelve if you can... Got your fancy dress? Remember: NO snoopers."

They roared off, and Jade crawled out, so stiff she could not stand, but she didn't even notice the cramps. Her mind reeled with what was planned on the river early the next morning.

Jade followed the shore around until she came to the beach. Though it was two hours before high tide, waves were worrying the seaweed and invading the rock pools. She squinted at the sun setting over the hills behind the house, thinking she should be getting back home. Still, she sat down on the beach and stared out to sea.

To the right, Point Mauri's high bulk glowed red-brown and olive in the last setting sun. The lighthouse was a golden wand flashing solar rays against the deep mauve of evening. The sea, a stretched hide scarred by whitecaps, extended eastward. Far out by the horizon, that odd cloud formation churned. Had it truly been created by Dr. Hagues? Its peak rose like a cone, high into the sky, tapering off into a wavering streak that stretched far up into the stratosphere.

Gazing at the water, she felt her mood shift. The air had changed. She waited for the rushing feeling of dizziness, but it did not come. The colors in the scene remained fixed. Yet something was happening related to the feeling she got with that dizziness. Almost as if the everyday world she was used to sprang more sharply into focus, but through a different lens. Things around her were clearer, yet seemed more dreamlike… subtly different. Staring at the ocean, staring, staring until her eyes began to weep, far out to sea, but closer than that storm cloud, she saw a tiny black point bobbing. As she watched, it moved nearer. Soon she was sure of it: The dark speck was coming closer, heading for Mauri Cove.

35.
CROSSING

Flung back out into the rain and the cold, to where the ocean heaved around their interlocked canoes, Kreh-ursh felt his own world harsh and cruel as waves piled high above the two craft. He could feel Taashou bending water, holding back the deluge that threatened to swamp them. He added his mind to hers in support, but she was glaring at him forcefully with both eyes and mind.

She spoke to make the force of her image clearer: "You must search! We must defeat this evil, cure it. Or our world will perish."

"How? Why me?"

Lightning flashed and thunder rolled low across the ocean, filling the silence her words caused.

"Your visions, we've been searching among the people... You are the one."

"Why...?"

"You must search out the cause... save your world."

"But I... How?"

She tossed a parcel into the bottom of his boat,

avoiding his gaze.

"Return when you have succeeded. Jaa-chuunaw Shahee-tohn. I name you Shahee!"

Then she was gone, throwing herself back into her own canoe, untying ropes and digging her paddle into the furious waves. For a moment, outlined on a wave crest, her wet body shone silver against the dark, limbs shining ghostly. Then her canoe dropped from sight. Kreh-ursh was alone again in the dusk, hurled deeper into the storm's fury. He focused on beating back the waves that heaved and shattered all around.

So it was a while before he noticed the pull of a singular, churning current. A deep unease took hold of him. When realization dawned, he was already lost. Faster and faster he spun. Using all of his mental skill, he sought to heave himself and his battered vessel free. It was useless. Fear wracked him. He was overwhelmed, yet knew not by what. The ocean rushed him along, frantic and unnatural. Waves reared, their crashing walls enclosing the canoe. Kreh-otchaw-oh galloped into a fathomless maelstrom, into blackness, a void, certain death. With every fiber he sought to keep Kreh-otchaw-oh whole, stopping her from battering herself to driftwood against the walls of this tubular cataract. The air shrieked and roared. The ocean boomed and hissed. Everything became dark, racing water. For an instant they entered a chill vacuum of space. He was plunged into deep cold. Something was wrenched, torn out of him—his heart or soul, he knew not, but a vital piece. It vanished into the black.

Then light came streaming back through the water.

They were careering down a wide, watery slope, his canoe spinning helplessly. The sea was gray-white, the light deep lilac. The tunnel spat them from its maw, and sky returned. Spray crashed, bursting in geysers all around, but the storm had passed over. While the sea still bucked, rough and angry, overhead clouds transmuted into a scarlet twilight. That was when he saw it behind him—an open maw in the ocean, slicing deep into the depths, yet simultaneously like a twisting chimney that spiraled away from the world in which he found himself. Was this it—the rift? He felt drained, weak, and horror-struck. Had he traversed it?

Looking ahead, he saw a distant shore. The sea was now calm, almost like a mirror. Kreh-otchaw-oh had been gliding fast across it, sail-less, without a paddle, without chants. Now she slowed and took to rocking up and down on the gentle waves that carried them along. For the sea had a different quality, though he could not work out what it was. It was as if this were a different sea, distinct in every sense. Bluer than he was used to, or grayer. Flatter perhaps and the air colder. But the biggest change was not the sea. It was that flat blur of land, not the lush shore he expected. Even from here, he could see that it was not his village coastline. In the distance it glowed, an olive band laden with puffy gold clouds. He was no longer in Shah, or in any place he had ever known, but in a strange, new land.

THE STORY CONTINUES

This is the end of *Through the Whirlpool*. Thank you for reading. The story continues in *Twilight Crosser* and *Lake of Stone*, available from the same retailer where you purchased this book.

Reviews and feedback help writers spread the word about their books as well as letting other readers know about great books. So, please, if you enjoyed this book, go to the website of your favorite bookstore and post a review.

If you'd like a taste of *Twilight Crosser*, Book II of the Jewel Fish Chronicles, read on.

HERE ENDS
Through the Whirlpool.

TURN THE PAGE TO READ THE
FIRST CHAPTER OF

TWILIGHT CROSSER

BOOK II
OF
SEEKING THE JEWEL FISH

I.
KREE-EH

On a day when Shah, the wide sea, was bright with sun and sparkles, flickering colors—green, blue, and gold—pulsated like heartbeats in the water. This was kree-eh: ribbons of delicate light that drifted in the current, reflecting the hues of the surrounding deep with magnified brilliance. If the sun was shrouded with cloud, the kree-eh strands appeared as nothing more than opal shimmers of mauve and orange within the ocean's gray heart. At sunset, they shone gold, lilac, and orange, though they softened to indigo and mauve by twilight. Yet as Shaamoh, the moon, lit the evening, they shone out like crimson and silver veins in the dark vastness.

"Enjoy her pretty colors, but never forget, she is alive, aware. Kree-eh is the mind of Shah, and only she can tell you what the ocean truly feels."

Geh-meer remembered this day, sitting at the old woman's feet on the beach at their village, Rrurd. They were mending the nets and baskets that the

Shahee, the sea nomads, used to fish from their canoes. To Geh-meer's young eyes—she was barely ten—the woman had seemed ancient beyond imagining. Yet Geh-meer sensed an undertone to their talk; she suspected it had to do with that serious matter of growing up, of becoming a woman. That really was why the proud old woman was there; Geh-meer knew enough to realize that she did not normally mend nets; she was one of the shahiroh, or sea callers, who lived on the volcanic island of Kaa-meer-geh across the bay.

Even after all these years, Geh-meer could remember the shariroh's exact words as she talked about the moon and the kree-eh:

"She, whom men call Shaamoh, the Pale Lady, truly has four names: Maataa when she is new, a waif barely visible in the sky; Shaamoh, as her body grows and assumes its shapely form; Sheehah when she takes on the pregnant glory of womanhood; and Sounaa as she curves and shrinks, bent by the weight of the knowledge she must bear in this world. But twice a year, as Sheehah, she brightens Hurm's rosy face to silver, and that is the time for harvesting kree-eh."

Hurm was the wide band of light that crossed their sky to the north. The shahiroh said she was once a moon who lay down in the sky and wept when her lover died, and her tears formed a river leading back forever to his grave beyond the horizon. In the daylight she shone a silvery rose and at night, magenta.

"How do you harvest it?"

"First, you thank Shah for her children. There is a special rite the shahiroh perform, before the Shahee paddle their canoes in a wide circle around a kree-eh bed. They sing to the kree-eh, asking it to come to them."

"I will be one of the Shahee one day, a sea nomad like my father. Then I may harvest it, too."

"You can be whatever you put your mind to be, child, but remember that the world owes you no favors."

Then her brothers, who were only four, woke the baby with their games, and she had to pick him up to comfort him. When she looked around, the old woman was gone.

Here she now was, barely seven years later, and though she had embarked on her sea-nomad-becoming, she had nearly lost it all. Sea-nomad-becoming was a private test, so to help another as she had helped Kreh-ursh, her fellow candidate, was forbidden. Yet it had been an emergency, hadn't it? She had saved him from being roasted by an ungrateful dragon. Even if it had nearly cost her the sea-nomad-becoming.

Returning to her own beach two days after having left, it had been a challenge to blanket her mind from the shahiroh who confronted her about her absence. Shahiroh were cunning with mind speech and could sniff a lie in a moment. She claimed she had got lost on the sacred island and had been wandering the slopes in despair. What she had done was right, she knew, even if it was against the rules. If she had acted on her last premonition, their friend Kaar-oh might still be alive. The forewarning that Kreh-ursh needed saving had come to her as soon as he had jumped from the great canoe. The farther the canoe traveled away, the stronger her foreboding became until it was throbbing at her temples, letting her focus on little else. Finally, she knew she would have to act.

As soon as she was dropped off, once the canoe was out of sight, Geh-meer began to run. Beach by beach, laboring over headlands, she worked her way back around the island until she reached the cove where Kreh-ursh had camped. She stayed in the jungle that night, seated in a tree fork, immersed in trance. Listening, not risking sleep. At one point she sensed a presence in the gloom and slowed every neuron to stillness. She watched, frozen, as Taashou—one of the senior shahiroh, the same old woman who had mended nets with her on the beach all those years ago— glided by beneath. The sea caller was wearing her ceremonial mask. That meant that another caller must be seeking Geh-meer far down the coast. Thereafter, the girl was scared to approach the beach, or to betray herself with even the slightest mental tremor. Only in the cold dawn, once the imperative to act became too great, did she dare to move. She had barely reached the thick foliage beside the shore when she saw Kreh-ursh, standing before her on the rocks, peering into the jungle gloom. Just as he pushed his way in, she slipped behind a tree. He seemed to sense her as she watched him harvest the sedative berries. She felt him cast around with his mind, but she was good, better than he at that skill. She dropped into a trance where she would not betray the tiniest mental activity. Soon he relaxed. He went looking for soap moss before returning to the beach. Hidden in the undergrowth, she watched him sedate the lesser dragon that had been brought low by the poisonous mud, and begin to clean its feathers.

Kreh-ursh would make a good Shahee, she knew, one of the best. Strong, intelligent, and sensitive to the life code, the rash boy who had been her companion in training for the last year seemed within two tide cycles to have grown into an adult. Perhaps it was because of his friendship with Kaar-oh that she had thought of him as a child. But he was barely a year younger than she was. Here on Zjhuud-geh, he was a man.

Feeling slightly silly, and believing that her trip here had been wasted, that she must violate sea-nomad-becoming no further, she was turning to leave when it came. The dragon raised its head—she saw it a moment before Kreh-ursh and mind-punched with all her force. The flame flashed past Kreh-ursh's scalp. The monster roared again, and again she mind-punched, both their minds acting in unison to turn its head. At the second attack, Kreh-ursh scrambled backward out of range, retreating toward the jungle. She also retreated, knowing he had sensed her. Turning to check where he was, she saw him just within the foliage line, watching the lesser dragon. That was when she made her mistake. The huge reptile was flapping its wide wings on the rocky shore. Silhouetted by the bright sea, Kreh-ursh stood, tall and square shouldered, watching the dragon. She was captivated, too—it was a beautiful sight. Kreh-ursh turned and saw her.

"Geh-meer!"

She ran.

PURCHASE

TWILIGHT CROSSER

IN PRINT OR EBOOK AT
WWW.POBLESECBOOKS.COM

K. EASTKOTT

Born on a South Pacific island, from his first foray into *The Hobbit* at ten years old, through writers such as Ursula K. Le Guin and Anne McCaffrey, K. Eastkott spent his formative years submerged in fantasy and science fiction. At nineteen he set out to discover the world and spent the next twenty-odd years living in and moving between countries such as Spain, Australia, New Zealand and England. "Seeking the Jewel Fish" is his first fantasy series. He writes arts commentary and contemporary fiction as Kevin Booth.

You can get loads of free stuff and stay updated with K. Eastkott and Poble Sec Books by signing up to our mailing list at:
www.poblesecbooks.com
Facebook: www.facebook.com/K.Eastkott
Twitter: @PobleSecBooks

Red, Black and Blue

Jessie Pyne
Print ISBNs
Amazon print 9780228637875
Ingram Spark 9780228637882
Barnes & Noble 9780228637899
BWL Print 9780228637905

Copyright 2025 by Jessie Pyne
Editorial Supervisor JD Shipton
Editor Nancy M Bell
Cover artist Michelle Lee

Dedication

To: shrewreading, eeyore9990, animentality, beka-tiddalik, brosequatz,shenko, katyakora, robininthelabyrinth, oneiriad and all the other Tumblr users who contributed to The Villain Wrangler thread, on which this novel is based.

Acknowledgements

BWL Publishing acknowledges the Government of Canada and the Canada Book Fund for its financial support in creating the Canadian Historical Mysteries collection.

BWL Publishing acknowledges the Province of Alberta for their ongoing support through the Alberta Publisher's Cultural Industry Operating Grant.